I0831518

AWKWARD IN TROUBLE

AN AWKWARD NOVEL

RACHEL RHODES

Awkward in Trouble

Rachel Rhodes

First published 2019

Copyright text ©

All rights reserved

The moral right of the author has been asserted

Cover design by Canva

Edited by The Writer's Block

"Chloe is such a slut!" Megan announces, dropping into the chair beside me and taking a huge swig of champagne. I follow the line of her narrowed gaze to where the company secretary is dancing on a black-boxed speaker, her hands roving all over her body, while most of the IT department gather eagerly around to watch.

"I wouldn't talk if I were you, Megs. She's not the one banging the boss."

"Shhhh!" Megan casts a furious glance around, checking that no-one is within earshot. "I've put an end to all that crap!"

"Since when?"

"I made a resolution yesterday morning."

"It's been a whole forty-eight hours? I'm impressed."

"This time I mean it," she insists and, although I know better, I find myself hoping that she does. Megan and I have been inseparable, ever since we both joined the sales department for Focus Media four years ago. Focus is an advertising company and, between us, Megan and I handle public relations, advertising, and media marketing for some of the biggest firms in the country. Megs is the complete opposite of me, and not only in character. She is dark where I am fair, and her blue-black hair is long and sleek, a shiny curtain that falls halfway down her back, whereas my hair is white-blonde and cut in a messy bob. I was going for get-up-and-go, but most days my hair gets up and goes without me. I've been trying to grow it out.

Megan's eyes are the color of chocolate – the real dark stuff, not the cheap kind. My own are a dirty Smurf blue, and, given that they dominate most of my face, could really afford to be a bit more impressive.

We both gaze across at Chloe as her performance increases in tempo.

"Dave the whizz-kid has the most enormous hard-on," Megan remarks drily, and I give a screech of laughter. Dave looks a bit like Steve Carrell in the *40-year-old Virgin,* and he has the personality to match. I don't think he's ever had a girlfriend. Megan laughs along with me until Jack Pendleton enters the room. Then she sobers instantly, leaving me cackling alone like a maniacal hyena. I give her a kick under the table but miss, stubbing my toe on the table leg instead.

Jack is the Company Director, young for the position at thirty-seven, married with two children – aged seven and nine – and too handsome for his own good. He glances around the room, shakes his head at Chloe, who has progressed to a spectacularly uncoordinated floss, and then his eyes come to rest on Megan.

"Don't do it," I murmur, thinking that if the heat in Jack's gaze is anything to go by, Megan's resolution is about to go up in flames.

"Oh God, I can't help it, Emma!" she sounds forlorn as Jack looks away. "I mean, *look* at him."

"He's married, Megs," I point out.

"Not happily."

"They all say that when they want leg-over. Ask him to leave his wife."

"He can't. He says he couldn't bear to leave the kids, at least not while they're so young."

"God, what a cliché." I take a slug of champagne. It's not that I don't respect my boss. Jack is an extremely astute businessman, and he is fair and pays us well. I do respect him, I just don't like him very much, and I hate that he has this hold over Megan. I can understand the physical attraction, given that Jack looks like a young Benedict Cumberbatch, but I know it's not going to end well.

"Hey, new guy!" Megan shrieks, and I turn my head to see the new sales executive who joined the company last week, making his way toward us. He hasn't been assigned to a team yet, so the jury's still out as to which Accounts Manager he will be reporting to.

"Hi Megan, Emma," he nods at each of us in turn and then pulls up a chair.

I return his smile. "It's Oliver, right?"

"At least one of you remembers." His hazel eyes crinkle at the corners when he smiles.

"New guy has a nice ring to it, I think," Megan teases. "But if you insist, Oliver it is."

Oliver chuckles as he leans over and refills our glasses. He's probably only a year or two older than I am, twenty-nine, thirty at most. He has nice hands, I note, as he sets the champagne bottle back in the ice bucket. I notice hands. Hands and eyes. And Oliver has a nice pair of both.

"Are office functions always like this?" he asks, gesturing over his shoulder at Chloe, who is now weaving around Dave like a Siamese cat on poppers.

"With *her*, it's always like this," Megan says. "I suggest you keep your head down, Oliver. Chloe loves fresh meat."

"Thanks for the warning." He grins again, and I find myself smiling too.

Megan has stopped paying attention. Once again, I follow the line of her gaze and I'm not surprised to find Jack at the end of it. He inclines his head discreetly toward the door and without waiting for confirmation, walks through it. I've barely opened my mouth when Megan is on her feet.

"Do me a favor and keep Emma company," she tells Oliver, swooping up the half-empty champagne bottle. "There's something I need to take care of." She winks conspiratorially at me and heads for the door.

Oliver watches her leave, a bemused expression on his face. "What was that about?"

I shake my head, draining my glass. "It's safer not to ask."

"Right." He flags down a passing waiter and orders another bottle of champagne and a light beer.

"So, are you married?" he asks, but it sounds more as though he is simply making pleasant conversation than prying.

"Divorced." I hold up my bare left hand as proof.

"Ah," he holds up his own. "Snap."

"What happened?" I ask.

"She left me for someone like Chloe." His face is deadpan, and I choke back my laughter until I see the amusement in his eyes.

"I'm sorry." I don't really know how to respond, but he just shrugs.

"I'm not, although I was a little jealous at first. Her girlfriend had the most incredible boobs."

"They could've at least given you a preview."

"That's what I said."

"Do you have any children?" I ask.

"No, thank God." His eyes widen as the obvious thought occurs to him. "You?" he asks, far more somber.

"One. A little girl – Alyssa. She's four."

"Beautiful name," he says, accepting the bottle from the waiter and setting it in the empty bucket.

"Thank you. It suits her."

"What happened?"

I take a moment to consider the question. My standard response is a simple, "it didn't work out" but the champagne has loosened my tongue.

"He drank too much."

"Ah," he nods thoughtfully, although there is no fake pity in his honest, open gaze. "My dad was an alcoholic. It's a disease, they can't really help themselves."

"I know, but when you have a child to consider, your tolerance goes out the window."

"Understandably." He raises his beer. "Well, here's to new beginnings for both of us."

"I'll drink to that."

An hour later, with the buzz of the champagne still warming my body, I cast a quick glance around for Megan. She's still missing – as is Jack. So much for Megan's resolution. I check my watch. It's time I checked on Alyssa. "I need to fetch my purse," I say.

Oliver gets to his feet a second before I do, old-school manners on full display. "I'll walk with you."

"No need. I need to make a call anyway. I'll be right back."

My office is down the hall, only a few doors down from Jack's, and I tiptoe toward it, praying I don't meet Megan and Jack on the way out. Jack's door is closed, his blinds drawn, and I heave a sigh as I retrieve my purse from under my desk. I'm bent over, my ass to the door when I hear a throat being cleared.

"Emma."

I whirl around to find Jack standing behind me, with an extremely attractive man at his side. Taking only a second to appreciate his tall, athletic build, mussed up blond hair and tanned face, and a few more to accept that he no doubt got an eyeful of my ass, I quickly turn my attention back to my boss. He looks agitated, and a small muscle is going in his cheek. I daren't ask him where Megan is, not with this stranger standing here.

"Yes, Jack?" I ask politely.

"Emma, this is Gregory Daniels. Greg, this is Emma Johnson. Emma handles the Nanosec account." He gives me a look that I assume is supposed to mean something important, but the champagne has addled my brain. Jack raises his eyebrows at me. "Mr. Daniel's company, Trivia, has just bought out Nanosec."

Oh! The penny drops. The new CEO of Nanosec, a company that spends over four million dollars a year with Focus. Nanosec is one of my key accounts which means that this man is now my biggest customer. What the hell is he doing at a private Focus function?

"I invited Greg to stop by and enjoy the festivities," Jack tells me, as if reading the question from my mind, "and I thought I'd introduce you."

I drop my purse on my desk, smile warmly and I extend my hand. "It's lovely to meet you, Mr. Daniels."

"Greg, please." He takes my hand, still cold from clutching my champagne glass, in his own, and it warms instantly. His green eyes hold my gaze for slightly longer than what I would deem appropriate and then dip almost imperceptibly to my chest.

"Greg," I correct, withdrawing my hand and feeling flustered. "I was actually going to give you a call tomorrow to set up an introductory meeting for next week."

"Next week sounds good," he nods, but his eyes are dancing with amusement. "Just give my secretary a call, and she'll set it up."

"Absolutely." I keep the smile plastered on my face. "I'll do that."

He gives me the ghost of a wink. "I look forward to it." He shakes my hand once more and then he excuses himself. As soon as he's out of earshot, Jack turns back to me.

"Emma," he begins, sounding sterner than usual, "there's something else I wanted to discuss with you. I'm afraid Megan Harris has been dismissed, her employment with Focus terminated with immediate effect. I am only telling you this now, *in confidence*," he continues as I open my mouth to interrupt, "because I know that you two are close." That's the understatement of the century – Megan is my best friend. "I do not want a scene," Jack warns, "and I expect you to handle this situation in the professional manner that you would display were it any other employee here at Focus."

"Why is she being let go?" I demand, keeping my voice low. Jack will not meet my eyes, and suddenly, I know. "Your wife found out, didn't she?" I hiss.

That gets his attention. "Emma," he warns, his voice low and threatening. "This has nothing to do with you. I am only telling you because I understand that your relationship with Megan may result in her confiding in you. However," he draws himself up to his full height, "you would do well to remember that I am your boss. And you will conduct yourself accordingly, or you will be charged with insubordination."

"This is bullshit!" I snap, knowing that there is not a damn thing I can do about it. "Megan is damned good at her job, and you know it!"

I'm surprised to see a flash of regret cross his features before his mask slips back into place.

"She is," he concedes, "and I'm not a monster, Emma. I have found Megan another position, she'll be on the same package, have the same benefits. In fact, she's been put on a higher commission structure, so this move will be good for her."

"Good for her?" I gape at him. "Really? How is losing her job good for her? And commission means nothing if you don't have any clients. She's worked her ass off to build up a base, and you're taking it away from her."

"Like you said, she's good at her job. She'll recover quickly," he insists. "And her salary won't change."

I can't even formulate a response, so I simply glare at him.

"I didn't want things to end up this way," he sighs. "But I have no choice."

"That didn't stop you before. You chose to have an affair without any scruples, so why let your conscience lead you now."

"Emma." It's my second warning, but I'm too angry to care.

"No, Jack, you know that I'm right. If Susan needs proof that it's over between you and Megan, why don't you leave instead?"

"That's not how things work."

"Really? And your wife dictating who you fire – is that how it works?"

"I never meant for it to end this way," he says, "but I will not sacrifice my marriage for a random fling."

I shake my head. "You're disgusting. You used Megan, and now she's paying the price."

"Megan was a mistake." He sounds as though he's trying to convince himself. "And this conversation is over. I will see you tomorrow." Before I can say another word, he turns on his heel and strides out of my office.

Fuming, I snatch up my purse and follow suit. I need to find Megan. I'm barely out of the door when I run straight into Oliver, who is holding two half-full glasses of champagne, the front of his shirt dripping with the balance.

"Oh my God, I'm so sorry!" I clap a hand to my mouth.

"That's okay," he shrugs, "I needed a hosing down, it's pretty hot in here."

"Seriously, Oliver, I'm really sorry," I stammer, grabbing a pack of wipes from my purse and pressing one against his sodden shirt.

"You keep those in your purse?" he asks lazily, his eyes crinkling again.

"I'm a mom, remember," I say, dabbing at his chest. "There, that's the best I can do."

He holds up the glasses. "I guess we'll need to refill these."

"I'm sorry, I can't. I have to go."

"Right now?" he asks, raising his eyebrows in surprise.

"Right now," I nod, stuffing the wipes back into my purse. "I'll see you on Monday."

I let myself into Megan's apartment with the key she gave me two years ago when she got tired of letting me in, and dump my purse unceremoniously on the table in the hall. The smell of champagne hits me as the sodden wipes tumble out of it. Muffled sobs come from Megan's bedroom.

Her dress has hitched up over her thighs, black lace panties on clear display. They're the kind you wear to be seen.

"He's a miserable son of a bitch," I say as I climb onto the double bed beside her and stroke her hair. Her body is wracked with sobs, her pillow soaked through. "You can take him to court, you know."

"No," she mumbles, wiping her face on the pillow and raising her head to look at me. Her brown eyes are bloodshot and her make up is smeared all down her face. I get up and cross to the vanity, soaking a cotton pad with cleansing cream.

"Sit," I instruct, and she gets up, crossing her legs beneath her and closing her eyes as I clean her face.

"I can't do that," she admits eventually.

"Why not?"

"Because it's not his fault."

"Oh, so it's yours?" I ask, anger flaring in my chest.

"No. Maybe. I don't know. I should have listened to you, Em. You told me this was going to happen."

"What did happen, exactly?"

"Susan found an old email I sent him. It was..." she pauses, trying to find the right word before she settles on "colorful." I can only imagine. "Apparently she went berserk, threw a stack of dinner plates at him and then demanded he get rid of me or she would take him to the cleaners."

"So, what, now he thinks she's just going to forgive him?" I snort with derision. "That if he does what she says they're just going to go back to playing happy family? That's never going to happen."

"You really think so?" Her face lights up with hope, and I toss the cotton pad aside.

"Megs!" I wail, "You're still hung up on him? Even after this!" I can't believe her. Jack just fired her, and she would still have him back in a heartbeat. She buries her face back in her pillow.

"I think I'm in love with him," she says in a small voice.

"Oh, Megan!" I feel helpless, unable to find the words to ease her pain.

"Where's he sending you?" I ask, after a long silence.

"Carter & Boyd." She lies down and stares at the ceiling. I do the same, and we lie side by side.

"Carter & Boyd are direct opposition to Focus," I say. "Why

would he do that? Why would he risk you taking business away from his own company?"

"He wants what's best for me," she sniffs. "I know you think he's awful, Em, and I don't blame you, but you didn't see him. He was devastated. He blames himself, says he's screwed up my career. He wants me to have the same opportunities I would have had if this hadn't happened."

I contemplate this for a while, saying nothing. It's a pretty grand gesture for Jack to make. He's hurting himself by sending someone as good as Megan into the opposition's hands. Maybe he's not as cruel as I thought. At the very least I might be able to tolerate being in the same room as him, which is not something I could avoid if I want to keep my job. And I really love my job.

It's after midnight when I finally feel that Megan has calmed down enough for me to leave her. I promise to check on her first thing tomorrow, and then I wearily descend the stairs from her apartment and hail a cab to take me home. I pay the sitter, pull on my old comfy sleep shirt, and climb into bed beside Alyssa. I pull her tiny warm body against mine and breath in her sweet scent – a mix of talcum powder, fabric softener and pure innocence. As always, it calms me, cementing me in this moment and overriding all the stress of my day. I kiss her cheek before closing my eyes, and then I drift off to sleep.

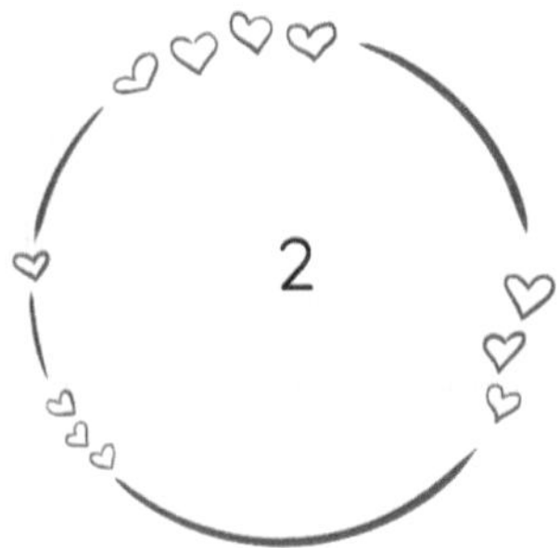

"Coffee," Oliver announces the following morning as he sets a Starbucks-emblazoned paper cup on my desk.

"You are a saint," I reach for it and scald my tongue with the first sip. "Who's bright idea was it to have the party right in the middle of the week, anyway?"

"You left in a hurry. Did you take the party elsewhere?"

I shake my head. "I wish. I had to leave for another reason. Girlfriend in need."

"Ah," he waves his own coffee in the air. "My ex-wife had that problem often. Although in her case, it was a little more literal." He heads out the door to his own office, and I smile despite myself.

I check my emails, and I am surprised to see one from Greg Daniels, sent at six this morning.

EMMA,

Further to our conversation last night, I propose we meet tomorrow (Friday) at 10.00 am. Please advise if this is acceptable to you.

Regards
Greg Daniels
CEO
Nanosec Technologies

TOMORROW? I thought we had agreed to meet next week. I quickly check my diary. I'm supposed to be an at internal sales meeting at 11, but I know Jack won't mind if I miss it.

DEAR GREG,

10.00 am is perfect, thank you for setting aside the time to see me.
Regards,
Emma Johnson
Key Accounts Executive
Focus Media International

I HIT send and check the rest of my emails, replying to each and making notes on those that I need to give more thought to. I wait a few minutes, but nothing new comes through, and so I pencil the meeting in my diary and pick up the telephone to make two calls. The first is to let Jack know that I won't be at the meeting tomorrow. The second is to check on Megs.

"Hey." Her voice is hoarse from crying.

"Hey," I reply, as brightly as I can manage, "how are you feeling?"

"Like crap."

"I'm sorry." It seems like such an insignificant thing to say.

"It gets worse," she sighs, "Jack's wife called me."

"Susan? What did she say?"

"She wants to meet me."

"Oh God, Megs. What did you tell her?"

"That I don't think that's a good idea," she sighs again, and my heart hurts for her. Megan is one of the happiest people I know. Usually.

"Have you spoken to Jack about it?"

"I can't. I'm terrified to call him in case she's around or sees the call register."

"Why don't you call the office?"

"No, I'm paranoid now. She could have spies anywhere. What if she's spoken to Chloe? Chloe hates me anyway, and even if Susan hasn't got her clutches in there, Chloe would think it's weird me calling, particularly after being fired. She'd probably tell the whole office."

"You're right," I admit. That's exactly what Chloe would do.

"Maybe you could...?" Megan lets the question hang, and I shake my head, even though she can't see me.

"No, Megs! I can't. Please, I don't want to get in the middle of this."

"I know it's difficult for you, but I just really need to ask his advice on how to handle it." Megan knows exactly how to push my buttons and play on my sympathy.

"I'll see what I can do." I concede, knowing I'm going to regret it.

"Thanks, Em. I really appreciate it."

"I'll chat to you later." I hang up and get back to work, wondering how on earth I am going to keep my promise to Megan as well as my own job.

Determined to research Greg Daniels as thoroughly as possible before our meeting tomorrow, I open a new browser window. It takes me less than a minute to sign into my Facebook account and another twenty seconds to find Greg's profile. It's set to private, so I can't see much, but I zoom in on his profile picture. He's on a mountain bike, covered in mud, and he's giving the cameraman two thumbs up. I click on the photos tab and a handful of images come up. A group of people in a white-water raft, one toppling out of the side as a wave of water hits the prow. A photo of Greg skydiving, his cheeks oddly distorted by the updraft. More cycling pictures, one where he is surrounded by a group of smiling women each wearing a matching pink shirt. I zoom in on the photo to read the words emblazoned on their shirt pockets: *Dirty Angels*. What the hell?

The more I look, the more I realize that I have nothing in common with Greg Daniels. He's a super-fit, super-competitive, overachiever. I prefer my achievers moderately adequate, and my idea of exercise is leaping over discarded Lego while cleaning the house.

Green tea, I think wryly. I bet he drinks green tea and snacks on Goji berries. In an act of defiance, I take a huge gulp of my coffee. It's ice cold.

I'm so absorbed in my stalking that I almost miss it when my phone pings. It's a text from Megan: *Did you speak to him?* I gaze dejectedly out of the window, then I push back my chair and head out of the door, taking a sharp left turn.

"Come in," Jack barks when I knock on his office door. I push it open and stand uncertainly in the doorway. Jack is at his desk, bent over a stack of paperwork and scribbling furiously, but he glances up when I enter and peers at me over his reading glasses.

"What is it?" He asks suspiciously. Usually, I just buzz him from my office like I had earlier.

"Um..." I take a few steps into the office, closer to his desk, "Jack, I was wondering if I could ask you a question. It's about Megan."

"I thought I made this clear to you last night, Emma," Jack interrupts furiously. "Megan is no longer employed by the Focus Group, and I have no wish to discuss this matter any further."

"It's not that – I mean, I'm not here to try and get her job back or anything." I wave my hands helplessly in the air. "She asked me to come," I say eventually. "Your wife called her."

Jack gets up without a word and closes the door. He takes off his glasses and pinches the bridge of his nose. "Susan called her?"

"Yes. She wants Megan to meet with her, and Megan obviously

doesn't know what to do. She doesn't want to cause any more trouble."

"How is she holding up?" His voice has lost all trace of irritation. Now, he sounds weary and concerned.

"She's your wife, you'd know better than I."

"Not Susan. Megan. How is Megan doing?"

The question is so unexpected it throws me for a loop. "She's okay," I reply. "She just wants to speak to you. I think she'd want that even if Susan wasn't hounding her for a meeting, though," I say pointedly, my message crystal clear. Jack smiles, and it's the saddest thing I've ever seen.

"Tell her to go ahead and meet Susan," he says, to my utter surprise. "I know my wife," he explains, "she won't leave Megan alone until she gets what she wants."

"What should Megan tell her?"

"The truth," he says simply, "I don't expect Megan to lie for me, Emma."

I nod and let myself out of his office, mulling over his unexpected thoughtfulness. This is the second time that I have been witness to Jack's feelings, and I'm starting to think that Megan is not the only one who was so affected by their relationship. It doesn't make me feel any better to suspect that Jack may care far more deeply for Megan than he's letting on.

I text Megan to let her know what happened, omitting my suspicions about Jack's feelings, which would only add fuel to the fire, and then I get back to work.

AFTER A BUSY DAY, I weave my way through traffic. My parents' house is only a few blocks away from my own, a sweet little two-story house with a grey roof and a blue front door.

When Alyssa was born, Max and I had stayed in an apartment in the city, but after the divorce, I'd moved out to the suburbs. It was well worth the extra half hour of traveling every day to see Alyssa playing outdoors, and I'd wanted to be closer to my support base. My mom and dad are a huge help; they fetch Alyssa from preschool, take her to the park, play with her in the garden, and do all sorts of fun things that I don't always have the time to do. My mom invariably almost always cooks dinner for the both of us, although sometimes I take mine to go.

"It's me!" I call as I enter through the kitchen door. My mother is standing over the stove, waiting for the kettle to boil. "Hi, mom." I kiss her cheek.

"Do you want some tea?" she asks.

"No, I'm good, thanks. I grabbed a coffee on the way home."

"How was your day?"

"Long." I grin. "Where's Ally?"

"They're in there." She points in the direction of the sitting room, where I find Alyssa and my dad playing dominoes.

"Mom!" Alyssa leaps up at the sight of me, knocking half the dominoes across the table.

"Hey, baby!" I scoop her up and twirl her in the air, kissing her neck until she squirms in my arms. "Did you eat?" I ask her, as I bend down to kiss my dad on the cheek.

"I did. Grandma made broccoli." She sticks out her tongue in disgust.

"Broccoli is good for you." I tap her on the nose and set her back down.

"I drawed a picture of us," she says coyly, trying to distract me.

"Drew," I correct automatically. "Oh wow!" I take it from her and can't stop the warmth that suffuses my cheeks as I look down at it. She's holding my hand under a wax-yellow sun. My parents stand beside us, their dark hair such a contrast to mine and Alyssa's. My mom meets my eyes over the drawing.

"We spent all afternoon on that," she says.

"It's beautiful. Definitely one for the pinboard."

"Your supper's in the warmer."

"I'm not staying, I've got a big meeting in the morning."

"Give me a second, I'll decant it for you." She disappears back into the kitchen.

"You okay, pumpkin?" my dad asks. "You look tired?"

"Long day," I reply. "Nothing a good night's sleep won't fix."

Mom comes back holding a plastic container, and I accept it gratefully before giving her a hug and my dad a farewell kiss on the cheek. I grab Alyssa's bag and head for the door. "We'll see you guys tomorrow!" I call over my shoulder. Alyssa trails along happily behind me.

An hour later Alyssa is bathed and ready for bed, and I manage to put my feet up for the first time today.

"You didn't eat all your broccoli," my daughter reprimands, glaring over my shoulder at the plate on the coffee table.

"Don't tell Grandma." I smile, and she narrows her eyes, sensing weakness.

"Can I have ice-cream before I go to bed?"

I pull her over the sofa and onto my lap. "Tell you what. Why don't we *both* have ice-cream before we go to bed?"

"Don't tell Grandma?" she asks, her dimples prominent as she smiles slyly.

"Don't tell Grandma," I agree, kissing her nose.

Twenty minutes later, I read her a bedtime story and tuck her into bed. She clutches 'Raffy' tightly to her chest and closes her eyes, utterly content, and my heart swells at how far she's come. After the divorce, it took months before she would sleep in her own room. Raffy is a stuffed toy giraffe that I bought for her as a baby. He is worn and faded, but she cannot bear to be separated from him, even now. I smile as I remember the time one of his legs fell off, and how I had to sew it back on while frantically trying to console her. When she'd finally calmed down, she had examined my stitchery, narrowed her eyes and announced that grandma would've done a better job. She hadn't asked my mother, though, and my uneven stitches remained.

At about nine o'clock my phone pings beside me. I frown as I reach for it. Who would be messaging me so late? A second later my question is answered. It's my ex-husband, Max.

Can I pick Alyssa up tomorrow night? I have tickets to see Cinderella at the Play Theatre.

I quickly type my reply: *I don't think that's a good idea. Let's stick to the arrangement. You can collect her on Saturday morning.*

I see him typing almost immediately. *I got great seats. The tickets cost me a fortune.*

I heave a sigh and feel the familiar fatigue settle over me. *Why did you buy them in the first place? You know you are only permitted day visits with A?*

There's a short pause, and then a new message comes through. *I didn't think it would be a big deal. She's my daughter too, Emma.*

Always Emma when he's taking me to task. I fight the urge to scream at how quickly the conversation took a turn for the worse. Instead, I hit the call button.

Max answers almost immediately. "Hi, Em."

I keep my voice calm. "Hey. Listen, I'm sorry about the tickets, but the judge did say we should stick to the agreement."

"Yeah, Emma, I hear you, but it's just one damn night."

"Max, please, let's not get into an argument."

"Who's arguing?" he counters, and I'm relieved to hear that he sounds sober. "I have really great tickets. For *Cinderella*," he emphasizes as if I don't know who that is. As if I didn't buy Alyssa the whole dress-up outfit for Christmas last year. "Ally will love it, what's the big deal?"

"The big deal is that I don't want you having her overnight. And I don't need to explain why, you know my reasons. They're the same reasons the judge decided on no overnight visitation to begin with."

Max is silent for a long moment and I cringe, expecting his temper to flare, as it always does. Surprisingly, when he replies, he sounds calm and amiable. "Okay, point taken. How about this. How about I fetch her at six, take her to watch the show, and then drop her straight back home after? The show is two hours plus an interval, so we won't be later than nine."

I consider this for a moment. Alyssa *would* love it – she's crazy about Disney princesses, and despite everything that happened between Max and I, she adores her father. And he has been trying, he spends as much time with her as he can and in the year since the divorce, I have never known him to be anything but sober when he's with her.

"I won't even get her an ice-cream on our way back," Max coaxes. "Straight home."

I cave. "Okay, that sounds fair. I'll let her know in the morning. You'll fetch her from my folks, then? At six?"

"Perfect," he says, and I can hear the delight in his voice. The knot in my stomach eases ever so slightly. Max has his faults, but he's a good dad.

"Great, I'll see you tomorrow."

"Tomorrow," he confirms. "And Em, thank you."

I hang up the phone and stretch my arms. It's getting late, and I have a busy day tomorrow. I pack Alyssa's bag, carefully folding her Cinderella dress, and feeling grateful that I opted for one size up last Christmas. It still fits perfectly. I pack her lunch for school, stowing it in the refrigerator before I switch off the lights, and pad down the hall to my room.

Sleep eludes me. I just can't relax. A part of me is furious that I agreed to Max going against the court order, and the other part of me is berating that part for being such a cynical bitch. I try to read to distract myself, but the words blur, running into one as my eyes droop. I give up, slamming the book down on my bedside table and reaching for the switch on my nightlight. My gaze falls on the frames on my bedside table.

In the first, Alyssa is laughing outright at the camera. It's not the best photo of her, her hair is a tangled mess and she has paint on her clothes, but I love it. The second photograph is of me with my parents. I'm riding my dad's shoulders and my mom is smiling up at me. It was taken only a few months after they adopted me, and mom says it's her favorite because it was taken the first time they heard me laugh. I avoid looking at the third photograph. The silver-framed image shows a pretty blonde woman on the beach, shielding her eyes from the sun, her curls blowing in the breeze. I can't face it tonight. Instead, I switch off the light without looking at it, and whisper softly, *Goodnight Mom.*

"Mr. Daniels will see you now," the platinum blonde at reception announces. She eyes me with cold indifference as I get to my feet.

I glance at my wristwatch as I make my way to the large double doors at the end of the hall. It's 10.00 am, on the dot. At least Greg Daniels is punctual. As I reach the doors, they open from the inside, and Greg smiles down at me, his blue eyes warm.

"Miss Johnson, welcome. Tracey, two coffees, please." He steps aside and gestures me in. I have been in this office plenty of times before, when the previous CEO was in residence, and I am struck by the changes in decor. Gone are the Persian rugs and the dark mahogany furniture. Instead, the walls are painted a dove-grey, and an enormous white shag-pile rug covers most of the floor. Greg's desk is enormous, but he directs me to a plush white leather sofa instead. I perch primly on one end, and he takes a seat beside me, lounging gracefully, his arm resting along the back.

"Thank you for taking the time to see me," I say, feeling strangely awkward at the informal setting.

"It's my pleasure," he replies, "I've heard only good things about your services."

"That's nice to hear."

He drums his long fingers on the sofa near my hair and regards me curiously.

"Look," I say, rising to the silent challenge, "I know why I'm here. I know that a new broom sweeps clean, and all that. I'm sure you want to explore all avenues and possibly make some radical changes here at Nanosec – it shows that you're actually doing something. I also know that you no doubt have a few weak spots in your expense budget, but I'm here to prove that I'm not one of them." I pause, and he nods his head, an invitation for me to continue. "Mr. Daniels, I *know* Nanosec, I know your policies, I know your systems, and more importantly – I know your people. I've done a fantastic job with your advertising and marketing over the past two years and, more importantly, I've hugely increased your brand recognition." He's smiling at me, but I'm not sure if it's encouragement or simple amusement. I shake my head, "What I'm trying to say, very inarticulately, is that you should give me a chance to prove myself before you start requesting comparatives." I stop, eyeing him patiently. "I'm done," I add when I realize he's still waiting.

"You think I asked you here to tell you I would be shopping around?" he muses, a small smile still playing around the corners of his lips.

I blink in confusion, feeling more and more out of my professional comfort zone. "It's what I would do," I say.

"What if I told you that I asked you here because I wanted to see you again?" he asks boldly, just as the door opens and Tracey enters holding a tray. Her eyes shoot daggers at me, and I flush to the roots of my hair as I realize that she heard his last comment. Greg, on the other hand, is completely unfazed, grinning down at me and not even glancing away when Tracey puts the coffees down on the table, with far more force than necessary.

"Thank you, Tracey." He waves her airily away. He waits until the door closes behind her before he speaks again. "Believe it or not, Miss Johnson, I did my research *before* we purchased the majority stock in Nanosec. I've seen the figures, and I already have a fairly good idea of who's not pulling their weight. I also know which of our service providers are worth their weight in gold, and you most definitely fall into that category. So, no, I didn't call you in to let you know that I would be seeking out comparatives. I called you in because I wanted to see you again and this was the easiest way to do that."

I regard him steadily. "Please," I say teasingly, "tell me how you really feel."

He laughs out loud. "What are you doing this evening?"

"I have no plans." I take a sip of my coffee, a part of me dreading where this conversation is headed and the other part ecstatic.

"I'd like to take you to dinner."

"I really don't think that's a good idea. After all, you are my client, and this could potentially cause a problem down the line."

"You mean once I've had my wicked way with you and moved on, and you have fallen completely and utterly in love with me?" He remarks, deadpan.

I really like this man. He has my sense of humor. I adopt a suitably solemn expression.

"Yes, then."

"That's understandable." He takes a sip of his coffee and pretends to ponder this dilemma. "Let's say, for argument's sake, that we find we don't enjoy one another's company. I'm not one to let my personal life interfere with my professional life, and I don't believe you are either. If it makes you feel any better, you could bring a briefcase full of reports, and we could treat it as a business meeting?"

"Why on earth would you want to take me out?" I ask. "We don't even know one another."

"I know what I want, and I didn't get to where I am by being hesitant. You might think I'm forward, but I prefer to think of it as being decisive."

"I actually like decisive," I admit, thinking of Max, and how much easier things would have been if I had followed my gut instinct. "Decisive is good."

There's a knock at the door. Tracey is back. "I'm sorry to interrupt, Mr. Daniels, but there's an urgent call from Tokyo on line two."

He gets to his feet. "I'm sorry, Emma, but I have to take this." I'm happy to note that he really does look sorry.

"Of course." I snatch up my things and follow him back to the door.

"Email me your address," he murmurs as I breeze past him. "I'll pick you up at 7."

By the time I get back to the Focus building, almost everyone else is on lunch. I head into my own office, shutting the door behind me, and wonder how I had taken such leave of my sanity. I agreed to go out with Greg – a client. How had that happened? I open a new email document, determined to cancel, but my fingers hover over the keyboard. What if I offend him? And truthfully, what harm is there in going? He's a client, and I've taken plenty to dinner. I have an entertainment allowance for that exact purpose. Besides, I *want* to go. I haven't dated since the divorce and Greg is the first man I've met that makes me want to consider it. Plus, it'll take my mind off Max taking Alyssa to the theatre and save me an evening of stressing about it. I hastily type up my address and hit send before I can change my mind, and then I get down to work.

I work hard. It's a big part of the reason I've been so successful and why my clients stick with me. I am so immersed in paperwork that, at first, I don't hear the knock at my door. When it becomes a firm rapping, I glance up from my notes.

"Come in!" I call, turning the page and highlighting Nanosec's new product range, which will directly affect their advertising portfolio.

"Hey, Emma!" Oliver grins, handing me yet another Starbucks coffee. Jack finally announced that Oliver will be reporting to Harvey, one of the other account executives. My initial dismay that he wouldn't be on my team was quickly replaced by relief that we could become friends, given that I'm not his direct boss.

"You are in serious danger of becoming my replacement Megan," I say, putting down my pen and stretching my neck from side to side. Oliver slouches into the chair across from me, looking at ease as he sips his own coffee.

"Just don't ask me to braid your hair," he teases.

"Not much to braid."

"True, but I could probably style you an awesome bed-head. What are you working on?"

"The Nanosec account. They've got an entire new range coming in, I'm going to have to completely rewrite their current proposal."

He's already halfway to his feet. "I didn't mean to interrupt."

"Please, sit. I could use the break."

He drops back into the chair. "What are you up to tonight?" he asks. He sounds only mildly curious.

"I actually have a date." I drop my voice conspiratorially, "with a *very* attractive, *very* powerful man."

"Ah," he nods knowingly, "I'm in the same boat. Except my date is female. And not very powerful. If I'm being honest, she's not even that attractive," he adds.

I laugh at his quirky sense of humor. "I hope it goes well."

"Ditto to you." He tosses his paper cup into the wastepaper bin. "I better go, Jack's got me reading through last year's reports to get me up to speed."

"Sucks to be the new guy," I tease.

"Tell me about it. Well, if you're at a loose end over the weekend, let me know. I'm always up for a coffee."

"Sure," I answer half-heartedly, my mind already on other things.

By 6.45 pm I'm dressed and ready. It's amazing how much quicker everything goes when you have the house to yourself and aren't being bombarded with questions from a four-year-old wannabe chaperone. I smile indulgently at the thought and then call my mother. Max fetched Alyssa right on time.

"Are you sure you don't mind waiting up for her?" I ask, for the hundredth time. In light of my date with Greg, I've arranged for Max to drop Alyssa back at my parents' place after the show, and they had agreed to have her sleep over. It means I won't have to rush and can let my hair down a bit.

At seven o'clock, on the dot, a dark blue Mercedes pulls up in front of my house. I hurry to the bathroom to do one final check of my appearance. My hair is clean and silky, if still too short, and my blue eyes look even bigger than usual, thanks to a new silver eye-shadow and at least three coats of mascara. I adjust the thin straps of my dress, which is a gorgeous aquamarine color. I bought it for last year's awards ceremony – the biggest Focus function of the year – but chickened out of wearing it at the last minute. A thin diamante belt fastens around the waist, and the skirt falls softly around my thighs and ends just above my knees.

A sharp rap reminds me that Greg is here, and I hasten back to the front door, switching off the lights behind me.

"Hi!" I smile up at him as I open the door. He really is gorgeous – possibly the most attractive man I have ever laid eyes on. His blonde hair is still in its deliberately mussed up style, and his strong jaw is clean-shaven. This close I realize that there are tiny flecks of green in his blue eyes, those wicked blue eyes that take in every inch of me, from head to toe, before he gives an almost imperceptible nod of approval.

"Shall we?" He asks, offering his arm.

"Let's." I smile, pulling the front door shut as I slip my arm through his.

Greg takes me to Luigi's. The risotto cakes are out of this world, the angel-hair wrapped prawns even better. As we move on to the main course, the red wine loosens my tongue, and the conversation flows. Greg is surprisingly easy to talk to. As I suspected, he's incredibly competitive and very athletic – doing everything from mountaineering to cycling.

"What do *you* do for fun?" he asks, filling up my glass and signaling the waiter. "A bottle of mineral water, please," he says, before turning his attention back to me.

"You're not having any more wine?" I ask, narrowing my eyes.

"I'm driving," he points out wryly. "So, fun?" he reminds me of his original question, and I wrack my brain. God, I don't do anything. My life revolves around work and Alyssa and trying to fit in the occasional leg wax, but I can't say 'nothing', and I hardly think that getting drunk at home with Megan while we burn the brownies for Alyssa's Baker Day will count.

"I swim," I hear myself saying. Sure, it's not the most exciting sport in the world, but at least I can pull it off. No fancy terminology or high-tech equipment. He never has to know that my version of a good swim is lounging on an air mattress, without wetting so much as a single toe, while drinking Pina Coladas and gossiping with Megs. To my relief, we're interrupted by the waiter, who sets down our main course.

As the evening progresses, I find myself becoming more and more attracted to this man. He is handsome, smart, successful, wealthy, athletic. He's almost too perfect. But I also realize that he is fiercely competitive, jealous by nature, and more than a little arrogant. He knows he's good looking and multi-talented. Somehow it only adds to his appeal.

We order coffee and I cave and order an exquisite Crème Brûlée. Greg declines pudding. No wonder he's in such good shape.

"Alyssa loves this stuff," I comment, as I take a spoonful. It literally melts in my mouth, and I close my eyes, savoring the smooth, creamy texture.

"Your daughter?" Greg prompts.

"Yes, she's four."

"My son is five," he states calmly, and I almost choke on my dessert.

"You have kids?" I hide my surprise behind a pleasant smile. Greg is at least 35, so I suppose it makes sense that he would have a child, and possibly have been married before.

"Just Jesse," he corrects.

"So, you're divorced?"

"Not exactly." He looks uncomfortable for the first time since I met him.

"What?" I ask, trying to stay calm. I'm sure there's a logical explanation. Maybe he's widowed. Oh God, that's it, he's a widow. I'm so insensitive, why did I bring it up?

"I'm still married," he admits bluntly.

"To your dead wife?" I blurt out.

He laughs, his eyes widening incredulously. "To my what?"

"Are you a widow?" I prompt, feeling confused and hurt.

"My wife isn't dead, Emma." He places his hand over my own on the table, and I realize that this has all been a set-up. He wants me to be his bit on the side, just like Jack with Megan. Tears of anger prick at my eyes and I set aside my plate, reaching for my purse. "Let me explain," his voice is low and inviting. I meet his gaze levelly.

"Greg, you ask me here on, for all intents and purposes, a date, and it turns out you're married. What explanation could possibly make that okay?"

"The one where I tell you that my wife and I have been separated for over two years and she's living with someone else?" he ventures.

I close my mouth. "Oh. Well, that might work, I guess." I purse my lips trying not to smile, but the effort is too much, and I grin unabashedly at him. "I'm sorry," I say, sounding anything but.

"Don't be," he shakes his head, signaling for the bill.

By the time we arrive back at my place, it's well after nine. Greg walks me to the door, and I lean back against it. I don't know if it's the wine or his presence that's making me feel a little unsteady on my feet.

"Thank you so much, I had a great time," I murmur, peering up at him and feeling ridiculously shy.

"Me too." He takes a step closer so that our bodies are almost touching. It's such an invasion of my personal space, but I'll be damned if I back away from a challenge.

"Well, I guess I'll see you this week?" I smile, and his gaze moves from my eyes to my lips. He doesn't say anything, but he lifts his hand and brushes my hair out of my face. My breath catches in my throat, a warm feeling spreading from deep in my belly through the rest of my body.

When his lips touch mine it's like an explosion. Feelings that I haven't felt in a very long time burst out of me, and my head feels fuzzy with longing. I hang almost limply from Greg's neck, barely able to stand my knees are so weak. He kisses my nose, grinning at the devastating effect he's having on me.

"You better get inside before I really take advantage of you," he murmurs, his voice heavy with the unspoken question. He doesn't want to go anywhere. I take a deep breath, throwing caution to the wind.

"Would you like to come in?" I manage, as his mouth comes crashing back down onto mine.

The moment is heating up fast and furious when my mobile phone rings. I pull away from Greg, using every ounce of my willpower, and reach into the depths of my purse. My mother's number flashes on the screen, and all thoughts of Greg are forgotten. I lift the phone to my ear.

"Mom?" She would never phone me this late unless there was an emergency.

"She's not home, Emma." She is trying to keep calm, but I can hear the underlying panic in her voice, "He hasn't brought her home and that bastard's not answering our calls."

"I'll call you back." I end the call and immediately dial Max's number. The phone just rings until it diverts to voicemail. "Son of a bitch!" I curse, immediately dialing again. "I'll kill him," I murmur under my breath and then, realizing that Greg is still standing here, I shake my head apologetically. "I'm sorry, my daughter isn't home yet, and my ex isn't answering his phone. You should go. Thank you for a lovely evening." I open the door and swing it wide, only half-paying attention. I'm already calling again, and I pace up and down as I listen to the dial tone.

To my relief, Max answers. To my dismay, he is slurring.

"Where is Alyssa?" I demand, grabbing my purse and heading out the door. I hesitate as I realize Greg is standing there, a hard expression on his handsome face. His jaw is twitching, and he hasn't moved an inch.

"She's with me," Max mumbles, "I figured there was no point driving her all the way back there and then fetching her again tomorrow."

"You don't get to change the plans, you bastard. And you've been drinking," I add, disgusted and terrified.

"Ah, that's not fair, Em. I only had a few beers."

"She's got no bag with her, no pajamas, no toothbrush." I snap.

"Stop being such a bore. She's fine, she's in one of my T-shirts."

"Whatever. Where are you?"

"We're at home. Chill out, everything's fine. I'll bring Ally back in the morning." His tone is final, as though the matter is settled.

"I'm coming to fetch her," I snarl, ending the call and tossing my phone into my bag. It immediately starts ringing.

"Dammit!" I check the caller ID and lift it to my ear. "Sorry, mom, I found her. She's at Max's."

"Do you need us to...?"

"No, don't stress, I'm headed over there now."

"Sweetheart if you prefer, your father can come with you."

"No, mom, thanks but that's not necessary. I'll call you when I'm on my way back."

"Where to?" Greg asks as I shove the phone back into my purse. His eyes are flashing. I hesitate for only a moment. I really don't want him caught up in this mess, but Max can be less than co-operative when he's been drinking, and I could use the support. I make my decision and nod at him, rounding the Mercedes and getting back into the passenger seat. Getting Alyssa home safely is my top priority right now, and if I never see Greg again because of this drama, well, it's a small price to pay.

The half-hour journey is tense, and we barely speak to each other, other than me issuing directions every now and again. We pull up outside of Max's apartment block, and I quickly climb the stairs and press the intercom button for 4C. I keep pressing it, over and over. It takes forever before I see finally get a response.

"Mmm?" Max's voice is thick and heavy with sleep. He must have passed out.

"Max, it's Emma. Open the door."

"Emma? What in Gods name are you doing down here?" He sounds so confused, and I still can't quite believe that he thought that his drunken explanation earlier would be the end of it.

"Max!" I yell, slapping the intercom unit as my anger boils over, "you open this door right now, or I'm calling the cops."

"You're making a scene, Emma! I told you she's fine. *We're* fine."

"Open the door!" My tone turns pleading as my desperate need to see Ally, to see for myself that she is okay, rears its head.

"I told you, I'll see you tomorrow," Max's voice is tight-lipped and menacing. "Now do us all a favor and fuck off." The connection goes dead. I blink in embarrassment and bite my lip, trying not to give in to the tears that are pricking at my eyelids.

I've already got my phone in my hands, intending to call the cops after all, when Greg steps forward, his face a mask of fury. As I watch, he presses the call button for 4B. The name tag reads 'Holloway'. After a short time, a woman's voice comes through the intercom, sounding half-asleep.

"Hello?"

"Ms. H?" Greg injects just the right pitch and slurring speech to sound convincingly like Max. "It's Max from 4C, I can't seem to find my keys, could you be a sweetheart and open up for me?" I can sense her shudder of contempt even from down here, but a second later the door clicks open. I am about to step through the doorway, but Greg bounds up the stairs ahead of me. I hasten after him, suddenly wondering if this might not have been the best idea.

By the time I get up the stairs, Greg is banging on the door of Max's apartment. I'm about to intervene when Max yanks the door open. Before he can even register his shock, Greg slams his fist into Max's nose. Max staggers back, tripping over a side table and falling heavily to the floor, his hand clutching his nose and covering his face. I don't waste any time. I rush into the apartment and down the passage to Ally's room. I find her awake in her bed, wide-eyed and shivering.

"Mommy?" She sits up as soon as she sees me. I pick her up off the bed, throwing the blanket around her, and scoop up her clothes and shoes. "I want Raffy," she moans, her lip quivering.

"We'll go get him, baby," I promise. Raffy is with her overnight bag at my parents.

I make my way back into the hall, where Greg is standing over Max as if daring him to get up. I think he's giving Max far too much credit, he looks incapable of standing. I shudder as I think of him driving Ally in that state.

"Who's the bodyguard?" Max stares at me through one glazed eye. Greg takes a step closer to me, and I give a tiny shake of my head. "I'll pick her up tomorrow," Max inclines his head at Ally, who has dropped her head onto my shoulder, her wide eyes taking everything in.

"No, Max, you won't." I declare, walking out the door. I don't look back.

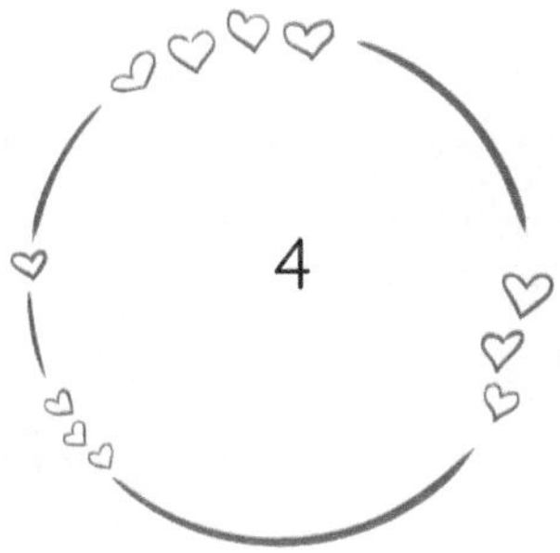

"If you wouldn't mind, I just need to pick up something from my parents' house," I tell Greg, keeping my voice low so as not to wake Ally. The interior of the car is warmer now – he had turned the heat up while I deposited her on the back seat.

"No problem." His voice is surprisingly gentle after the cold anger he displayed earlier. I call my mom on the way, and she is relieved to hear we are both safe. I explain that I'm going to just take Ally home, but that I need to stop and collect Raffy first. I hang up and direct Greg, leaving him in the car to watch over the now sleeping Alyssa while I run in to fetch the stuffed toy and the small Frozen backpack filled with Ally's overnight kit. I feel Raffy's matted fur beneath my palm. It's no wonder Ally couldn't settle. Max really doesn't know his daughter at all. I take a deep breath, determined to stay calm. Max is an asshole, that's why I divorced him. He can't hurt me anymore, or Alyssa. I went against my better judgment letting him take her out at night, but it won't happen again. Back in the Mercedes, I give Greg a tentative smile.

"Got it," I hold up the tattered toy and his lips pull up at the corners. When we pull up in front of my house, I open the back door and lift Ally into my arms. I maneuver the keys in my left hand, as I do so often when she falls asleep in the car. I hear Greg chuckle beside me as I fumble with the lock. He takes the keys from me and opens the door in three seconds flat.

"Thank you," I mouth, kicking off my shoes and padding down the hall to tuck Ally into bed. I slip Raffy between her arms and she clutches him to her chest with a small sigh. After five minutes, she still hasn't stirred, so I kiss her cheek and leave her to sleep. I find Greg in the kitchen making coffee.

"Thanks." I take the proffered mug gratefully and raise it to my lips, meeting his gaze over the rim. "So, I guess our date turned out to be a bit of a disaster?"

He comes to stand beside me and leans back against the counter. I can feel the warmth of his body at my side.

"Was his drinking the reason you got divorced?" he asks gently.

"Yes and no. We were very different, it probably would have ended eventually anyway. But if he wasn't drinking I might have hung in a little longer – the marriage may have limped along a few more years."

"He ever hit you?" It's such a personal question, I flinch, but I won't lie. I have nothing to be embarrassed about, or so my therapist told me.

"Only once."

He nods slowly, then turns and puts his cup in the sink.

"I should go." He clears his throat and turns to face me, then without warning, he puts his warm hands around my neck and pulls me to him. He tastes of coffee and I kiss him back, my head swimming with desire.

As the kiss deepens, he runs one hand down my left thigh and lifts my knee, cupping our bodies even closer together. I groan as his teeth graze my bottom lip, and his breath fills my mouth.

"You should go," I murmur. He nods, but neither of us makes any move to break apart. When he kisses me again, I rake my nails down his back. Greg groans and the sound only fans the flame of my passion. "Or, you could stay," I add, my voice hoarse with longing. After the stress of this evening, I crave the oblivion of sex. It's all the invitation that he needs. He picks me up and carries me, my legs wrapped tightly around his waist, all the way to my bedroom.

I WAKE in the morning and give a start. Greg is sleeping soundly beside me, and as I grab my phone to check the time, I hear Ally's bed creaking – a sound symbolic of her waking up.

"Greg!" I hiss, shaking him frantically.

"What?" He opens one eye. A lazy smile parts his lips.

"You have to go!" He gives me a look of pure astonishment. "I'm sorry, but Alyssa is waking up, and I don't want her to see you." I blush furiously – I can't believe I am asking him to do the walk of shame. I can only assume it's because he has a child of his own that he understands.

He eases himself out from under the covers and stretches uninhibitedly. I admire the view for a moment before he reaches for his clothes and pulls them on. I get up, pull on my robe, and slip my feet into my well-worn snoopy slippers. I open the door and peer through the crack. Ally is nowhere in sight. Praying she's still in her room, we hastily make our way down the hall and to the front door. "I'll call you later." He kisses my nose, grins, and turns for the door. His hand has curled around the handle when I hear Ally's voice right behind us.

"Mom?"

I freeze, wondering how I'm going to explain this, when Greg suddenly shuts the door, turning to face me and announcing in a loud voice. "Thank you for letting me in, Miss. As I said, my car ran out of gas just outside and I need to use your phone, if you don't mind?"

I gape at him, until his foot brushes my own.

"No problem at all," I say, playing along. "I'll get my mobile. This is my daughter, Ally," I add, smiling down at her. Ally narrows her eyes suspiciously. "Ally, this is..." I trail off, and he takes his cue.

"Greg," he extends his hand, and I shake it, "Greg Daniels."

Ten minutes later Ally is back upstairs in her room playing, and Greg and I are settled in the kitchen with coffee, supposedly waiting for a gas-wielding friend of his to arrive.

"That was some pretty quick thinking," I concede, still laughing over the morning's events.

"I took an acting class in college," he boasts, then, checking his watch. "I guess it's about time my friend arrived with the gas."

I watch as he quickly rinses his mug and sets it in the drying rack.

"About last night..." I say to the broad span of his back. He turns to face me, waiting.

"Yes?" he prompts when I say nothing further.

"I'm not quite sure what to say," I admit. "It's not exactly something I normally do."

"Which part? Taking your dates to your ex's apartment, or jumping into bed with them on the first night?"

I pretend to ponder the question. "Both, I guess."

He chuckles and then fixes me in that blue-eyed stare. "I want to see you again."

"Well, as long as you keep using Focus for all your advertising, you'll see me at least every fortnight, for sure," I tease.

He smiles lazily. "I was thinking maybe a little more often than that."

"How often?" I pretend to be contemplating.

"Often," he states simply, the word filled with meaning.

"I'll have to check my diary and see if I can carve out some extra time."

"I'm away until Tuesday, I'm competing in a cycling challenge. Could you come by my office on Thursday, say ten, and we can discuss it?"

"That sounds good."

He cocks his head, listening for the sound of Alyssa, still playing upstairs. Convinced, he crosses the kitchen to kiss me.

"I'll see you on Thursday."

I'm still grinning when I hear the BMW start up outside.

NOT FIVE MINUTES after he has left, the doorbell rings, and I open it without thinking.

"Did you forget something?" My smile falters as I gaze up into the cold, bloodshot eyes of my ex-husband. He's sporting a spectacular blue bruise around his left eye, and his nose is swollen above the grim line of his mouth.

"Max," I stutter, stepping forward into the doorway, barring him entry. Ally is still upstairs. "What are you doing here?"

"How dare you," he spits, his voice ominously low. "How dare you come into my home and take my child?"

"I beg your pardon?" I snap, my ire outweighing my fear. "You were dead drunk, and you had *our* daughter. What did you think I was going to do – leave her there?"

"I certainly didn't expect you to have me assaulted."

"Assaulted?" I smile sweetly, "I have no idea what you are talking about. You were hammered. For all I know, you tripped over your own feet."

"You think you've got this all neatly wrapped up?" he sneers, uncharacteristically aggressive considering he is sober. Max has always been a nice guy, save for when he drinks – it brings out the devil in him. "You will not keep me from my child." He takes a big step forward so that we are almost touching.

"Max," I press my hand firmly against his chest, trying to calm him down. "Don't make a scene. Please. You know I would never keep you from her unless I thought she was in danger. You were drunk, and in violation of the court order," I add, firmly but with no accusation. "She was cold and she had no clothes with her. I did the right thing." He hesitates, and a shadow of guilt passes over his face, which softens slightly.

"Yeah," he relents, "I guess that was pretty dumb. But you drove me to it, Emma. You're too damn uncompromising. She's my daughter too. I need to see her." That was the gist of it, right there. Max may have been a terrible husband, but he does love Alyssa and, despite everything, she loves him. I have never denied that fact.

"Then *earn* it, Max. Your behavior last night is proof that I can't trust you with her."

"Who was the guy?" he changes the subject abruptly. "The one you brought with you?"

"Just a friend."

"I don't want to see him again, Em. You bring him near me, I'm going to return the favor – you got that?"

"Got it," I agree – anything to have him gone. I am immensely relieved that Greg left when he did. Who knows what might have happened if he had still been here when Max showed up. "Look, Max, I know technically today is your day, but she's still a little shaken up about last night. Please, just leave it for today, until we've both calmed down. I'll drop her at your place next Saturday." I have no intention of ever leaving Alyssa alone with him again, but I need to buy myself some time to get the court involved. In the meantime, I need to keep Max calm, and not invoke his temper.

"Where is she?"

"Upstairs, playing."

He glances toward the stairs, deliberating. "Okay," he agrees finally, and I expel the deep breath I have been holding.

"Thank you," I say, meaning it. "And I'm sorry about your eye," I add, gesturing toward his face.

"Like I said," he replies, "don't let me catch him sniffing around here."

I WAKE up late the following morning, as is my custom on a Sunday. Alyssa is curled up in the small of my back, her warm body acting as a natural hot water bottle. She must have come to cuddle and fallen back asleep. I ease myself out of bed and tiptoe downstairs, retrieving the paper from the front porch and settling down on the sofa, a steaming cup of coffee in hand.

By mid-morning Alyssa is climbing the walls and desperate to go out. On a whim, I call Megan.

"Hello," she croaks.

"Hey," I chuckle. Megan would sleep until noon if she could. The joys of not having children. "How are you holding up?"

"Not good," she replies, sounding oddly stilted. "I met Susan last night."

"Oh shit. How did it go?"

"It was awful." She groans.

"Well, I have just the thing to cheer you up. We're going to the park. Get up, get dressed, and meet me there in an hour."

"Seriously?"

"Yes. Alyssa says she's missing you."

"Liar."

"Well, no, she didn't, but that's probably because she's forgotten who you are."

"I saw her at her ballet recital."

"That was over a month ago. Now get up."

"I'd rather just curl up and die."

"No, you wouldn't. You're Megan Harris, young, gorgeous, marketing-wizard extraordinaire. Oh, and you're going to be late – get moving. We'll see you in an hour."

"I hate you," she intones grumpily.

"I hate you more. Move your ass."

By noon Alyssa is playing on the playground and Megan and I are stretched out on the grass, enjoying the midday sun.

"It was awful," Megan moans, after relating her meeting with Susan. "She was just so devastated. I always thought of her as a cold-hearted bitch who didn't understand Jack, you know? But she adores him. Her heart is broken."

"Was she angry with you?"

"No," she shakes her head, her dark hair trailing over the grass behind her. "That's the worst part. She was so nice. She said she doesn't blame me – that he is ultimately responsible and the person she expected loyalty from."

"Ouch. So, does that mean she's going to leave him?"

"She says she can't because, despite everything, she still loves him."

"Shit."

"I know." She slumps forward, head in her hands. "Am I an awful person for wishing he'd call?"

"No," I console, squeezing her shoulder. "But I wish you'd told me things were this serious."

"I didn't expect them to be. It started out as a fling – the best casual sex I'd ever had."

"Too much information," I groan.

"Well, it was!" She smiles. "But then, I don't know, somewhere along the line it became something more."

"Have you heard from him?"

"Not a word. Has he said anything to you?" She is trying to be nonchalant, but she can't hide the desperate hope in her voice.

"Nothing, Megs, I'm sorry. But it's only Sunday."

"Yeah. They're probably having family time as we speak."

"Don't do that. Don't obsess over it. You need to move on with your life."

"You're right." She sits up straighter. "Tomorrow I start at Carter & Boyd. And my first item of business will be to screw every available man in the office."

"Not the best way to impress the boss," I laugh.

"I'll screw him too," she teases, "he'll give me a raise."

Monday flies by, and I'm slightly disappointed that I haven't heard from Greg, but I figure if he's out in the wilderness on his bike, he probably doesn't have the best reception. I pencil in our appointment for Thursday in my diary and log it into the electronic system for good measure. I contact my solicitor, who promises he will send through a court order application immediately, pressing for supervised visits only between Max and Alyssa. I feel a twinge of regret that it has come to this, but Max is spinning out of control, and I cannot allow Alyssa to get caught in the cross-hairs of his emotional issues.

"How was your date?" Oliver asks, appearing at my door after lunch, his auburn hair standing up at all ends.

"It was good," I smile, glancing up at him. "Yours?"

"Disastrous. She was at least forty, if a day, although God knows she did her best to hide it. I think she takes her make-up off with a chisel." He takes my smile as an invitation and comes into the room, lounging on the chair opposite my desk. "Oh, and she deliberately chose the most expensive items on the menu," he adds, outraged.

"Ah, one of those," I nod knowingly. "I suppose she gave you only a motherly peck on the cheek to express her gratitude.

"I wish," he slumps further down in his chair. "She grabbed hold of me like a sumo wrestler and sucked like a Hoover. I thought she might suck out my soul," he adds shakily. I burst out laughing.

"Well, I guess then I forgive you for not bringing me coffee this morning. You've been scarred. How did you escape?"

"I said I was going to get some Champagne and ran like hell."

"She could find you," I point out. "Did you tell her where you worked?"

"Yes," he sounds woeful. "Couldn't you maybe just tell her I died?"

"We'll figure something out," I chuckle. "What was her name?"

"Simone."

"Well if Simone calls and I happen to answer I'll make sure to let her down easy. So long as you promise never to forget coffee again. Deal?"

"Deal." He grins, getting to his feet, and then, almost as an afterthought. "Hey, you didn't tell me about *your* date?"

"We'll chat later, I have a few calls to make."

ON TUESDAY I seek Jack out, determined to have something to tell Megan when I meet her tonight for drinks. I know she's going to drill me and, given that I work only a few doors down from our Director, I may as well try and glean some information out of him.

"Jack," I knock softly.

"Come in!"

"I'm sorry to intrude," I begin, and then I trail off when I see Susan sitting opposite him, dabbing at her face with a tissue. "I'm sorry," I start backing up, "I'll come back later."

"No, no, come in," Jack looks grey with exhaustion, and I wonder at the emotional toll this whole thing must be taking on him. "Susan was just leaving." As she turns away from him, I notice a flash of anger cross her face, before she quickly composes her features and gets up to kiss him goodbye. She scowls at me as we cross paths and then shuts the door quietly behind her.

"What can I do for you, Emma?" Jack asks politely, resting on the edge of his enormous desk.

"Really, it's not the time," I mutter, wishing I had never come in here. Jack regards me steadily, waiting, and eventually, I cave under his scrutiny. "It's Megan. I'm so sorry to bring it up, but I'm meeting her tonight, and I know she's going to ask me about you. I know it's completely inappropriate, but I thought maybe you had a message I could give her. Something that will make her heart hurt just a little bit less?"

"You're meeting her tonight?" he asks.

"Yes. For drinks."

"Where?"

"*Buccaneers*, but that's not the point... wait, you aren't thinking about joining us, are you?" The look on his face makes it clear that he was thinking just that, but, as I watch, his expression changes into one of determined acceptance.

"No," he replies, "of course not. I'm sorry, Emma, that you've gotten caught up in this whole mess. Not to mention the pain I've caused my wife, and Megan."

"Was it worth it?" I can't help but ask him. There is something in the way he looks every time he mentions Megan's name. He doesn't answer me for the longest time. I'm just wondering if I should get up and leave when he focuses on me again, his face pained.

"Yes and no," he says. "If I hadn't started it, I wouldn't have to deal with these mixed emotions. I love my wife, but I can't seem to get Megan out of my head."

"You have to," I point out, feeling incredibly sorry for him. I can see now how hard this is on him, the toll it's taking, and my heart goes out to him almost as much as Megan. "You can't possibly carry it on, and Megan deserves to be happy. You need to let her move on with her life."

"I know," he agrees. "And I won't leave my wife, or my kids. I would regret it forever, I know I would, no matter how Megan makes me feel. Tell her that," he adds, pushing away from the desk and crossing the room to sit behind his computer. His expression changes. "I see you have a meeting with Gregory Daniels on Thursday?" he asks and I take it that the 'Megan' portion of our conversation is over.

"Yes," I reply.

"How do you feel about our retaining the Nanosec account?"

"Oh, very positive," I answer honestly. "Trust me – Nanosec is not going anywhere."

"Good," he nods. "In that case, I'll be coming with you on Thursday."

"With me? Why?" I ask. Jack almost never accompanies me to any client meetings. He trusts me implicitly. I'm just that good at my job.

"Because I'm the Company Director," he retorts snappily, "and Nanosec is one of our biggest clients. I'd like to touch base, unless you have a problem with that?"

"Of course not." I smile, cursing the fact that I scheduled the meeting into our electronic system. "Well, I have work to do, so, if there's nothing else?" Jack waves airily at the door, dismissing me, and I wonder how someone can be so personal one minute, and such a dickhead the next.

"SO THAT'S ALL HE SAID?" Megan asks, hungry for information.

"Yes," I admit, "he has feelings for you, but he won't leave her, Megs. Ever."

"So, he won't even call me?"

"It's better if you have no contact."

"That son of a bitch!"

"He's struggling," I try to explain. "This whole fiasco has taken a lot out of him. He looks exhausted, and I think Susan's giving him a harder time than he's letting on."

"What, so you want me to feel sorry for him now?"

"No, it's not that. But I kind of do."

"Oh my God. Are you crushing on Jack?"

"What?" I gasp, "Are you insane? He's my boss!" She pulls a face, and I quickly change tack. "What I mean is no. Not at all. I don't see him that way."

"He's an asshole." She shakes her head angrily. "An utter, bloody asshole."

"I don't think he meant to hurt you." I'm trying to calm her down, but it only riles her more.

"Well he *did*, Em, and, as my friend, I would expect you to be on my side."

"I'm not on anyone's side!" I exclaim. "I feel sorry for all of you, it's a terrible situation!" She doesn't look appeased.

"Are you sure you don't have feelings for him?" she asks, eyes narrowed suspiciously.

"I am *so* sure. Besides, I've met someone."

"What? And why are you only telling me this now?"

A part of me is wondering why I am telling her at all. I don't even know what's happening between Greg and I but I'm so desperate to convince her that there is nothing going on between Jack and I, that I blurt out the whole story.

"I don't believe it," she breathes when I'm done. "Who would've thought you had it in you. Go, Emma! Was he good in bed?"

"Marvellous," I grin, taking a slug of my Martini.

"Well, at least you know Nanosec isn't going anywhere."

"Not if I can help it. Jack would throw a shit fit if I lost their account."

Just for a second, a flash of something sinister crosses her face. "You won't." She says. "Not as long as Greg Daniels is in charge. When are you seeing him again?"

"Thursday. He's out of town, competing in some cycle race."

"Has he called you?"

"No," I shake my head, signaling to the waitress to bring me another drink. "But he's probably busy."

"Um-hmm," she raises a skeptical eyebrow. "Sure he is. When is he due back?"

"Today, actually."

"So why is he only seeing you on Thursday and not tomorrow?"

I get the sense that Megan's man-hating frenzy is spilling over to encompass the entire male population.

"Let's talk about something else, okay?" I say. "I don't want to jinx it."

"Okay, how about how I'm going to make Jack suffer?" She proposes, and I laugh. It relieves the tension slightly, but it is still there, lingering between us, for the remainder of our evening.

THE COURT ORDER comes through on Wednesday morning, far faster than I expected. I'm on lunch when my mobile rings and Max's name appears on the screen. I cringe, bracing myself as I answer.

"Hi."

"How dare you, Emma?" he sounds incandescent with rage. "How fucking dare you do this?"

"Max, calm down." I'm relieved that I sound calmer than I feel.

"Don't tell me to calm down. How the hell can you do this to me?"

"You gave me no choice after last weekend."

"That's bullshit!" he retorts. "It was a one-off, Emma, and now you want to keep me from my own daughter? You've gone too far!"

"I'm not keeping you from her!" I snap back, just as Oliver steps into my office, a perplexed frown on his handsome face. I lower my voice and turn away from him, my hands shaking. "You can still see her just as often."

"With supervision!" he roars. "So, I have to contend with your ugly mug every time I want to spend time with my daughter?"

"Essentially, yes," I reply, forcing a confidence I don't feel. Max has always had this effect on me – making me doubt myself – making me question whether I am doing what's best for Alyssa.

"Well, I think I'm going to report you, too," he threatens, "for the assault that you orchestrated."

"You deserved it," I point out.

"Possibly," his voice is ominously low, "but it should spark some doubt as to your apparent perfect parenting. You're no saint, Emma. In fact, the secrets I have on you would probably get social services very concerned over Alyssa's safety. After all, violence tends to be inherited. Maybe you're more like your old man than I ever gave you credit for."

"You leave my parents out of this, you son of a bitch!" I hiss, then, realizing that me losing my temper is exactly what he wants, I take a deep, steadying breath. "Do you really think that having Alyssa removed from my custody is best for her? To be taken into social services and shuffled from foster home to foster home until the truth prevails and they determine I am a fit mother?"

"You're going to pay for this," he replies, not answering my question.

"I'm doing what's best for Ally!" I yell into the receiver, "why can't you see that?"

The line goes dead as he hangs up on me, and I fling the phone across my desk, tears pricking at my eyes.

"Emma," Oliver's voice is low, "are you okay?"

I had all but forgotten that he was in the room. Embarrassed, I sniff loudly and clear my throat, forcing a smile.

"I'm fine," I insist. "Ex-husband problems."

"You want to talk about it?" he asks gently.

"Not really." He nods his head and turns for the door, but before he reaches it, he stops.

"I have a friend who works at social services," he announces, turning back to face me. "I heard you mention... well, if there's anything I can do to help, I'd be happy to give him a call." I hesitate, my pride battling my good sense. I need an ally, and some advice on how to handle things should Max make good on his threat.

"Actually, that might be very helpful," I admit, taking a deep breath. If I'm going to accept Oliver's help, he needs to know the truth. He takes a seat opposite me, his amber eyes warm and trustworthy.

"My ex took my daughter home without permission on Friday night. He was supposed to drop her at my parents, but he had a few drinks and decided to take matters into his own hands," I add, and Oliver's eyes widen in understanding. "Anyway, I applied for a court order so that he no longer gets unsupervised visitation."

"Ah," Oliver nods. "And I assume he's not taking it lying down?"

"No," I sigh, rubbing at my temples.

"Well, if the court has issued the order, I don't see that he can do much to oppose it."

"He wants to plant doubt that I'm a fit parent."

"Do you think he would do that? That's not going to do Alyssa any good."

"Max can be a bastard," I reply simply, by way of explanation. "Right now, all he wants is to hurt me. He won't think any further than that."

"But surely the court will realize this is just his way of lashing out at you?"

"Hopefully," I admit, "but there's more to it than that."

Oliver says nothing, waiting for me to find the right words, which of course, is impossible. There are no words to explain what happened.

"My father murdered my mother," I blurt out eventually. I hear his shocked intake of breath. There was no way he saw that one coming. "They were really happy for the longest time – he was the most amazing man, and we were very close. Then he lost his job when I was about twelve, and he started drinking. My mother had to go out and find work, and I think he really struggled with that. She must have met someone at the office, because she started coming home late, and they started arguing a lot. It spiraled out of control pretty quickly. She was always out, and he was always drinking, and when they came head to head, it got really ugly." I close my eyes briefly as I recall just how ugly. I can still hear the echoes of their fighting, like ghosts in my head that I can't shut out.

"Emma," Oliver murmurs tentatively, a world of compassion in that one little word.

"My mother eventually announced we were leaving," I state, opening my eyes and smiling sadly at him. "She had met someone, at work, just as we suspected. I'll never forget my father's response. He said 'You try, and I'll put you six feet under'."

"Jesus," Oliver murmurs.

"Two days later I came home from school with a friend. Their bedroom door was closed, and I figured my dad had passed out. By the time my friend left and it started to get dark, I was getting concerned that if my mother didn't get home soon there would be another epic row."

"Did your dad...?"

"He wasn't there," I interrupt, needing to get it out while I still can. It's been years since I've spoken about this to anyone, barring my therapist, after Max and I got divorced. "She was. It got to the point that my concern for her safety overthrew my fear of an argument and I went to wake him up so that we could go looking for her. She was on the bed, surrounded by half-packed suitcases. Her face was blue, and her body was cold, but I tried to revive her anyway." I pause, the memory becoming so clear that for a moment I can't go on. Oliver makes to stand, but I stop him. "I'm fine," I gesture him to remain seated. "The police arrived shortly after. My father had turned himself in. I wish they had been an hour earlier, though. I wouldn't have found her if they had."

At this, despite my protests, he makes his way around the desk, pulling me to my feet and taking me in his arms. He pulls me against his chest and for a moment I let the sound of his heartbeat, steady and solid, comfort me.

"I'm sorry," I mutter, feeling embarrassed.

"For what?" he asks, incredulous. I step away, smoothing my hair nervously and trying to regain control over my emotions.

"It was a long time ago," I stammer, pulling myself together, "and I ended up in foster care with the most amazing couple, who treated me as their own. They adopted me and gave me an amazing life. My mom still cooks me dinner most nights." I force a laugh. I can't believe I just told him all of that, and then I remember his friend in social services and why I started telling him in the first place. "Anyway, Max knows, obviously, and he's threatening to use it to cast doubt over my character and cause trouble."

"I'll call my friend right now," Oliver promises. "He'll clear it all up. You don't need to worry about anything."

"Thank you," I take his hand and squeeze it, not knowing how else to express my gratitude. Oliver glances down at my hand and I quickly let go. A small silence follows and then he moves away from me, toward the door.

"Emma," he calls, when he reaches it.

"Hmmm?" I glance up to find him regarding me intently, as if not sure how to voice what he is thinking.

"Your father...?" he lets the question hang in the space between us and I smile reassuringly, letting him know that the question doesn't offend me.

"He's in a federal prison, serving a double life sentence for murder in the first degree."

"The first?" he frowns, and I can understand his confusion. Ordinarily, my father would have been tried for a crime of passion.

"I testified that he had threatened to kill her," I explain sadly, "it was enough to try him for premeditated murder."

ONLY WHEN OLIVER is gone and my office door closed firmly behind him, do I collapse back on my chair, my legs shaking. I haven't seen my father since the day they led him away in court. I was thirteen years old. Although fifteen years have passed, it still feels like yesterday, and the haunted, hollow-eyed look he gave me as they led him away is crystal clear in my mind.

Determined not to dwell on it any further, I turn my attention to my computer and check my emails. I find a message from Greg, which would make me feel better if it weren't just a short note to postpone tomorrow's meeting.

Emma,

Something has come up that I need to attend to. It can't wait. Can we reschedule for Monday afternoon?

I slump back in my chair, my whole body deflating. Even though he hadn't called yesterday when he arrived back, I had still been holding out hope that he would, at least before our appointment tomorrow. Now, the very first correspondence that we have since he left my house on Saturday morning is to delay our next meeting. It doesn't inspire much confidence that he wants to see me again.

I set my personal feelings aside and type up a response.

Greg,

No problem at all, Monday will be perfect.

I trust you had a wonderful trip.

I stay at my desk for the next half hour, hitting the refresh button every few minutes, but no reply is forthcoming and I have meetings scheduled this afternoon. I type up a quick email to Jack to let him know of the postponement and then I shove my chair back and stride from the room.

"Hello!" I call as I push open the front door.

"Mom!" Ally comes rocketing down the stairs and vaults into my open arms just as my mom emerges from the kitchen. She has flour on her nose.

"You've been baking again, mama?" I ask, chuckling, just as the smell of her famous shortbread reaches me. "I hope I get to take some of that home?"

"Obviously," she says.

"You ruin all our fun," my dad grumbles as he descends the stairs, looking forlorn. "I waited for ages!" he adds, scooping Alyssa up as she shrieks with laughter. "You didn't find me!"

"I found you now," she points out happily.

"True," he acknowledges, leaning over and kissing my cheek. "How was work, sweetheart?"

"Busy." I follow my mom into the kitchen.

"I keep telling you, you work too hard," she admonishes, opening the oven and setting a tray of golden shortbread onto a board on the kitchen table. I grab a piece and pop it into my mouth, savoring the warm, heavenly crumbliness.

"Good?" Mom asks with a smile.

"Divine," I reply, through a mouth filled with shortbread.

My mother, Janet, and my father, Reggie, fostered me after my mother's death. I had been a withdrawn, troubled teenager, and yet, somehow, they had managed to see past the walls I had built up and had coaxed me out of my protective fortress. "Life is for the living," they'd reminded me gently, never pressing me, but slowly smothering all my anger and despair with kindness. They had been unable to have children of their own and had fostered several, of various ages, but for some reason, they had chosen me to adopt permanently. They had never fostered again, preferring to dedicate all their love and devotion to me instead, and give me as normal an upbringing as possible. Somewhere along the way, Janet and Reggie had become my parents – become mom and dad – and I loved them both just as much as I had my biological parents. Their greatest delight is Ally, who is the apple of their eyes, and who has them both wrapped around her little finger.

"Are you staying for dinner?" My mom asks, and I smile across at her.

"Dinner would be great."

We get home a little later than I'd planned, and I carry Ally to the house, careful not to wake her. I leave the front door open as I carry her to her room, needing to go back to the car to fetch my purse. Tucked up in bed, she snuggles Raffy, smiling in her sleep, and I gaze down at her in wonder. Sometimes the love I feel for her seems like it might overwhelm me – this beautiful, fragile child, who completely and utterly captivates me. It's still hard to believe that after all the terrible ugliness in my life, I was rewarded with something so exquisitely beautiful. Kissing her cheek, I brush her blonde hair off her face and make my way quietly from the room, pulling the door shut behind me.

The smile still lingers on my face as I descend the stairs, my mind slowly shifting back into work mode. Determined to spend at least an hour on a new campaign I've been working on, I move toward the door and give a screech of fright as a tall figure looms over me.

"Oh my God, Max!" I gasp, my hand clutching my chest. "You scared the crap out of me. What the hell are you doing here?"

"I want to talk to you about this." He waves a stack of documentation under my nose, no doubt the court order papers, and I catch the sour ferment of beer on his breath.

"You've been drinking."

"Oh please. Don't start your shit with me."

"You need to go," I walk past him to stand at the still open door. "We can talk about this when you're sober." Max doesn't move, and I see the spiteful glint of satisfaction in his eyes. He loves to antagonize me when he's been drinking – to prove what a big man he is. Forcing myself to stay calm, I try to focus on the good times we shared, before he started drinking so heavily. Max had been a good husband, and he had loved me unconditionally. I had accepted long ago that he wasn't the same man anymore, but it was still a tragedy that he had become this awful person.

"Please, Max. I don't want to fight with you."

"You started it," he retorts, throwing the papers toward me. I watch as they flutter to the floor.

"I'm sorry, but I did what I had to do. One day you'll thank me – when you realize that I kept Ally safe."

"I would never harm a hair on her head!" He moves closer to me, trampling the discarded papers underfoot.

"Not intentionally," I admit, digging in my heels. "Don't you think I *know* that? But you're not the same when you drink, Max. You promised you'd never hurt me either, remember?" He hesitates, a flash of guilt crossing his angry features. He *had* promised. When the drinking had started to get out of hand and I began to fear the worst, he had assured me that he would never, ever hurt me. That I was his whole world. He had been sober at the time, and he had meant it. But just two weeks later he had come home drunk and spoiling for a fight. Our argument had escalated rapidly, and before I knew it, he'd dealt a brutal left hook to my cheek. I had suffered a black eye and a fractured cheekbone, which was agonizing but fortunately required no surgery.

I hadn't given Max a second chance. I refused to be one of those women who didn't learn the first time. I had seen first-hand what alcohol could do to a man, had watched my kind, gentle father become a monster, and I had watched my mother hesitate before leaving him. If she had just left, she might still be alive today. So, I didn't hesitate. I left Max the very next day and filed for divorce. He had begged and pleaded, sworn that he would never do it again. Eventually my quiet, earnest, "I will not become my mother," had silenced him, and he'd signed the divorce papers.

Without Ally and I there to curb his drinking, Max had spiraled out of control faster than I would have thought possible. My concern for his safety was tempered by the fact that Alyssa's safety came first, and in his defense, he was always sober on the days he had visitation with her. I had never smelt so much as a whiff of alcohol on his breath when he returned her in the evenings, and for a long time, he had often stayed after dropping her and had dinner with us.

It was only recently that things had started to change. At first, it was barely noticeable, and I might have missed it if I hadn't been paying such close attention. Max had dropped Alyssa home one Sunday afternoon, and his eyes were slightly redder than usual. He was also too careful with his words, and speaking in a stilted, formal manner. I had gone berserk, threatening him with legal action, and berating him mercilessly for driving our daughter, even if only mildly intoxicated.

He had taken it gracefully, and for a few weeks, things had gone back to normal. Convinced it was an isolated slip, I eased up on him, trying to give him the benefit of the doubt. It turned out to be my undoing because less than a month later he made the same mistake. That had been three weeks ago, and then last weekend had been the sleepover incident. It was enough. Three strikes and you're out, in my opinion. I would not let empathy cloud my judgment.

Max sways slightly as he peers at me, and I take advantage of his temporary guilt to set the record straight.

"The order stays," I announce, "not because I want to hurt you, but because I cannot allow you to hurt Alyssa. I'm doing this for you, too. You would never live with yourself if something happened to her. If you can't be responsible enough to make that call, then I have to make it for you."

He says nothing, just gazes at me with an unreadable expression on his face. He doesn't seem angry, but a muscle is going in his jaw, and his hands are balled into fists at his sides.

"You want to talk about responsibility?" he murmurs eventually, his voice so low I can barely hear him. "What about yours? You had a responsibility to me, to our marriage and the vows we made. You broke up our family, Emma. I could've stopped... I would've stopped."

"When?" I cry. His twisted reasoning infuriates me. Max refuses to be held accountable for his own actions. "When you broke another bone? When I ended up in a hospital? I gave you so many chances, I begged you! We were a family, Max, and *you* fucked it up! You wouldn't stop! You *couldn't* stop!"

A dark shadow crosses over his face. For a long moment, he simply stares at me, the monster inside him barely leashed. Then he releases a shuddering breath. "Well I guess now I have no reason to," he murmurs, and just like that he stalks past me and out into the night.

I shut the door and rest my back against the warm wood. Sinking to the floor, I pull my knees up against my chest and drop my head. I had mourned the loss of my marriage a long time ago, but when I catch glimpses of the man I had once loved so deeply, it still makes my heart hurt.

AT TEN AM the following morning, I am staring unseeingly at my computer screen, all too aware that right now I should be walking into Greg's office. I'm far more hurt by the fact that he hasn't called than I want to admit. My budding relationship with Greg had been the silver lining in a sky full of grey – something bright and colorful, the euphoria of possibility.

"You up for a visit?" Oliver's dark head peeps around the door frame.

"So long as you have coffee in those hands you're hiding." He steps around the door frame and into my office, bearing two steaming mugs.

"Have I told you I'd be lost without you?" I ask, perking up considerably.

"I have a hidden agenda," he admits, setting the coffee down on my desk and curling his long frame into one of the stiff chairs opposite me.

"Oh, really? And what is that?"

"I'm hiding," he grins, "Simone's called my cell twice, and I haven't answered. She's bound to call here next."

"You want me to screen her?" I laugh, picking up my mug and blowing on the coffee to cool it.

"No, just give me sanctuary for a while. She's stalking me. And I'm far too nice a guy to tell her off." The fact that he's right makes me smile, but his next words make me laugh out loud. "By the way, you can't purse those lips like that and expect me to keep a handle on things." I almost choke on my coffee, and as I try to swallow it down, he grins goofily.

"Your knack for innocent flirtation is a gift, you know."

His phone starts to ring, and he winces, showing me the screen. "She's not going to give up."

Lifting my handset, I dial reception. "Chloe," I say as she answers, "Oliver's in my office, he'll be here a while. Please forward all his calls to my extension."

"Sure," Chloe answers breezily, and I hang up.

"You are a lifesaver," Oliver sighs, lifting his legs up onto the desk and getting comfortable.

“So are you,” I reply dryly, tipping my mug at him.

“What are you up to this weekend? Any plans?” Oliver asks as we both watch the phone expectantly.

“No,” I shake my head. If Greg wanted to see me, he would’ve mentioned it in his email. I gathered from his curt message that I would only see him again on Monday. I haven’t even bothered to tell him that Jack will be coming with me, it hardly seems to matter considering the meeting will no doubt be all business.

“Ah,” Oliver frowns sympathetically, “your date didn’t work out either?”

“Not exactly.”

He regards me steadily for a while and then his face lights up.

“Let’s go out!” he proposes. “We can console each other over the pitiful state of our social lives. We’ll drink to our singlehood, long may it last! I propose Saturday – do you think you could get a sitter for Ally?” The fact that his first thought is consideration for my single motherhood status is so startlingly kind that, for a second, I simply stare at him, barely noticing the phone, which has started ringing. Oliver cringes, clapping his hands dramatically over his eyes, groaning, and I snap back to the task at hand.

“I’ve got this,” I laugh, holding up my hand for him to be quiet.

“Hello, Emma Johnson speaking.”

“Hello?” A breathless voice murmurs nervously, “Is Oliver there, please?” Simone sounds far younger than she must be.

“May I ask who’s calling?”

“My name is Simone.”

“Simone, I’m so sorry, but Oliver had to fly upstate for a few days to negotiate a new contract. He’ll only be back mid next week.” Oliver is pressing his lips together to keep from chuckling. “Next week?” her deceptively youthful voice squeaks.

“I’m afraid so,” I reply curtly. “Is there anything I could perhaps help you with?”

“N... no,” she stammers, “that’s okay, I’ll call him next week.” Without another word, she hangs up.

"Well yes, actually I do have his direct line number," I speak into the handset, and all the blood rushes from Oliver's face. "It's five five one..." I continue as he shakes his hands frantically, signaling me to stop. I place the phone back into its cradle, chuckling. "She's gone," I concede, and he slumps back into the chair in relief. "She hung up. She's going to call you next week."

"Well, at least I don't have to worry about her for a few days," he sounds ridiculously pleased.

"You can't avoid her forever – you know that, right?"

"Yes, but maybe if I avoid her just long enough, she'll get the message and find a new victim to sink her claws into."

"I wouldn't bank on it. She doesn't sound forty, by the way."

"Right? She's a practiced predator." I burst out laughing, and Oliver joins in. "So, about this weekend," he continues eventually. "Think you could get someone to watch Ally?"

"My folks would do it, I don't even have to ask."

"Well then, no excuses. Shall I pick you up at seven?"

I shift in my seat. For him to fetch me feels too much like a date.

"I'll meet you there," I say. "And I'll ask Megs to join us. She could use a night out." His face falls for just a fraction of a second, so fast I might have imagined it.

"Awesome!" he declares, getting to his feet. "*Zack's* at seven?" He is already making his way toward the door. "It's where all the cool peeps hang out these days. Or so I've been told."

"We'll be there."

"Hey, new guy!" Megs kisses Oliver when we arrive at the bar, leaving a flaming red lipstick mark on his cheek.

"Hi," I say, wiping it off with my thumb after I give him a quick hug. "Sorry we're late, it took forever to catch a cab."

"No problem, I took the liberty of ordering you a drink," he gestures at the table where two Martinis lie in wait.

"Dirty, just the way I like it," Megan croons, swooping her's up and taking a huge slug.

"Why am I not surprised?" Oliver grins. Megs waggles her eyebrows at him. Megan has always been a flirt, but for the first time, I find myself a little irritated by it. Throughout the evening she never misses an opportunity to lay her red-taloned hands on Oliver, giggling at his jokes and giving him long lingering eye-meets.

As a result of their endless conversation, I drink more than either of them. Listeners always drink more, I think stupidly, my head buzzing as I raise my hand at the nearest waiter and signal for a refill.

"Maybe you should take it easy?" Oliver murmurs, his eyes meeting mine.

"What are you, my mother?" I chuckle, pushing his shoulder and almost unseating myself.

"Emma's a big girl," Megan interjects, drawing Oliver's attention back to herself.

"I guess," he shrugs, turning away, but I am all too conscious of his concerned glances back at me.

"I'm going to dance," I announce, feeling a little embarrassed. I *have* had far too much to drink. The stress of these past few weeks is catching up with me. Swaying, I move toward the pulsating dance floor, which is filled with shiny, beautiful people. Oliver and Megan join me a moment later, and we form a crude triangle, laughing and spinning as we move in time to the up-tempo music.

Oliver takes it in turns to spin us, his hands remarkably steady. Megan is writhing around him, rubbing her body against his and lifting her arms above her head in that sexy, slutty way that I've never been able to master. My moves are far less coordinated, but I shuffle around like a baby elephant, having just as much of a good time. Most surprising is the fact that Oliver is not responding to Megan's advances. In fact, he deliberately moves closer to me, raising his eyebrows in fear. I stifle a laugh as I step closer to murmur in his ear. "It'll be okay. She's not Simone, and she's not as scary as she seems."

The next thing I know, his head shifts to the left and our mouths meet. I'm not sure who initiated the kiss, but the sensation is warm, heady, and familiar all at once. It lasts only the briefest of moments, and then Oliver pulls away, his hand catching me by the elbow as I stumble backward.

"I'm sorry," he apologizes over the loud music, his hazel eyes searching my face. "Are you okay?"

"I'm fine," I smile, embarrassed.

"I didn't mean to..."

"It's okay," I insist, brushing it off. "Really, Oliver, it's fine."

Megan's face is a priceless mask of indignant outrage, but she quickly composes herself, shrugging nonchalantly.

The evening continues without incident, and I share a cab with

Megs on the ride home. Oliver is charming as ever, and there is no awkwardness after our impromptu kiss. He bustles us into the waiting cab, unfazed.

"What was that about?" Megan whirls on me the second the cab door closes on us.

"What was what?"

"Oh please, don't you 'what was what' me! That kiss!"

"That was a simple case of far too many Martinis."

"Oliver didn't have too many Martinis," she points out wryly.

"What is that supposed to mean?"

"I don't know if you were paying attention, but he hardly drank a thing all night."

"He must have," I insist, but now that I think about it, I wasn't really paying attention.

"A couple of beers at best," Megs confirms.

"Well, it was nothing," I insist. "A mistake. It won't happen again."

"What about Greg? Are you guys still a thing?"

"I have no idea," I admit.

MY DOORBELL RINGS the following morning, and I moan, clutching my head as a stabbing pain shoots through my skull. Ally spent the night at my parents, so I'm alone in the house, and not particularly in the mood for company.

"Go away!" I groan as I descend the stairs to another chiming ring of the bell. I yank open the door, and the sunlight hits my eyes like needles. Blinking against the bright light, I find Oliver standing on my porch, holding two enormous coffees. He looks revoltingly refreshed.

"Morning," he grins. Wordlessly I take a coffee and pad back inside. "How are you feeling?" he asks as he follows me through to the living room. I slump onto the sofa, cradling my coffee against my chest like a lifeline.

"Hungover."

"I figured you might be."

"Aren't you?" I ask, narrowing my eyes slightly as I recall Megan's words from last night.

"I feel like someone put me in the drier overnight on spin cycle," he counters. "Listen, I'm not going to stay, I just wanted to apologize, again, for what happened last night. I don't know what got into me, but I blame it on the alcohol."

"Me too," I agree. As far as I can remember, it wasn't as if Oliver forced himself upon me. I don't think either of us initiated that kiss – it just kind of happened.

"As long as things aren't going to be weird between us" he begins, but I cut him off.

"Oh God, no. You're like, the only person I even talk to at work – you're my person, my Christina Yang." The fact that he laughs at this and understands the *Greys Anatomy* reference only proves that we're destined to be friends. "Besides, who else is going to bring me my daily caffeine fix?"

"Who indeed," he replies, looking relieved but not entirely convinced.

"You want to stay for a bit?" I ask. "I only have to fetch Alyssa this afternoon. We could watch a movie?"

He hesitates, trying to decipher whether I really want him here, or whether I'm just being polite. I give him my most sincere smile. "Okay, sure," he says eventually, taking a seat opposite me. "What are we watching?"

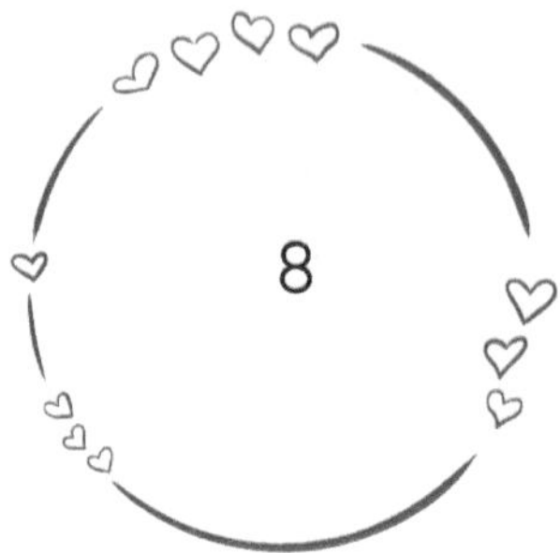

8

By Monday afternoon I'm angry enough that I feel no nerves walking into the Nanosec building. Greg's complete lack of communication has made it clear that our relationship was a non-starter and I will not allow my personal feelings to jeopardize my career. I know that my work is unparalleled, and I'm ready to prove it. I spent the whole of Saturday developing a cast-iron marketing proposal that not even Jack could punch any holes in.

Tracey ushers us to the soft leather sofas across from her desk, far more friendly now that I have a handsome man in tow. "Mr. Daniels will be with you shortly. May I offer you anything to drink while you wait?"

"No, thank you," I reply, while Jack simply shakes his head. We spent most of the morning closeted together in my office and, mercifully, Megan didn't come up once. I think it is safe to say they are both moving forward with their lives, although my relationship with Megan seems to have taken the brunt of the damage this whole mess has caused. There is something up with her that I can't quite put my finger on. Vowing to pop in on her after work and see how she's doing, I get to my feet as Greg's office door opens and the sound of laughter reaches us.

Jack's astonished intake of breath beside me is completely justified, and my own polite smile vanishes as I recognize Megan's voice a second before she appears in the doorway. What is she doing here? I rack my brain, trying to remember if she mentioned having any reason to call on Nanosec, but I come up blank. A sick feeling settles in the pit of my stomach. Greg's arctic blue eyes meet mine over her dark head, and his own mouth hardens into a grim, determined line.

"Thank you for your time, Ms. Harris," he drawls charmingly, "I'll be in touch." Megan pirouettes toward us, her high heel hitting the ground before she registers Jack and I, standing directly in her path. Shock and worse, hurt, flash across her face as she meets Jack's gaze, but she quickly composes herself.

"Jack, Emma," she nods curtly, refusing to meet my eyes, and then she sweeps past, her heels clicking on the expensive marble floor. Jack is visibly stunned, whether from seeing Megan again, or specifically, from seeing her *here*, I cannot tell, but I smooth down my skirt and pull at his elbow as we follow Greg into his office.

Greg is professional and courteous, but there is an ugly set to his jaw, and the greeting he bestows upon Jack is noticeably warmer than the perfunctory nod he offers me.

My presentation takes twenty minutes, during which I offer a non-stop dialogue as to the advantages of my new proposal, which is a good thing because it keeps me distracted and allows me the opportunity to compose himself. Greg watches me intently, but I refuse to be flustered, and I answer all the questions he fires at me afterward with confidence. Inside, I am seething. How dare he contact the opposition when he promised me that Nanosec would continue to do business only with Focus. *And after he slept with you*, a little voice in my head adds.

"Thank you both for coming," Greg says, after we have concluded the business at hand. "I'll need some time to mull things over, but your proposition seems sound enough. I'll try to get back to you before the week is out."

That's it? I want to scream, *that's all you have to say?*

"Thank you for your time, Greg," Jack shakes his hand warmly, but I can tell that his calm exterior is feigned. Not surprising when I assured him that the Nanosec account was secure, only to find Megan here upon our arrival and Greg deciding he needs time to mull things over. I concentrate on packing up my things, shoving diagrams and paperwork roughly into my presentation folder. Eventually, I can avoid it no longer, and I turn to find Greg standing right behind me. He extends his hand, and I take it, finally looking up at him. I can't hide the hurt that I know is reflected on my face. His eyes widen in surprise, but I retrieve my bag and hoist it over my shoulder.

We are almost at the elevator when he catches up to us.

"If you don't mind, Jack," he calls, "I'd like to speak to Miss Johnson alone. I have a few more questions I'd like her to answer."

Jack seizes the opportunity as a positive sign and nods his head exuberantly.

"Absolutely, take all the time you need. I'll meet you back at the office," he adds meaningfully.

Greg doesn't look at me once as we walk back toward his office, but as we pass Tracey's expansive desk, he calls out to her. "Tracey, two coffees, please." Only when we are finally alone, and he has shut the door behind us, does he take a deep breath and turn to face me.

"How could you?" I can't help the blatant accusation in my tone. I don't know if I'm more hurt by his personal rejection or his professional one, but I decide to focus on the latter. "How could you set up a meeting with Carter & Boyd before you'd even given me the chance to present? I've worked my ass off for this company, for four years. Since signing with Focus, Nanosec's revenue has increased threefold. I didn't deserve this!"

"On the contrary, you *asked* for this," he replies cruelly, his jaw clenched so tightly it's a wonder he can get the words out.

"I beg your pardon?"

"You had the account!" he's almost yelling now, "you had it to begin with, and there was no way I was going to move it anywhere. I know how hard you've worked, and your service speaks for itself, but you left me no choice! How do you expect me to be taken seriously as the new CEO if I'm seen to be making decisions based on my personal life?"

"What?" I have no idea what he's talking about.

"You went and blabbed about us to your *opposition*, Emma! How arrogant are you? Telling Carter & Boyd they would never shift Nanosec's business because you were sleeping with the boss?" He is so insanely angry that I take an automatic step back, my mind whirling as I try to comprehend what he's saying. "If you screwed me to retain this account, I don't even want to know what you do for all your other clients!"

"What are you talking about?" I stammer, as the door opens and a highly excited Tracey steps through it with a tray.

"On the table," Greg barks, and she quickly deposits the tray. "That will be all," he adds menacingly. Her face falls, but she darts from the room, closing the doors behind her.

Greg runs a hand over his clean-shaven jaw and takes a deep breath before continuing. "I'm talking about getting a call from Carter & Boyd on Wednesday morning accusing me of exercising nepotism in the running of a fortune five hundred company. And seeing as I certainly didn't kiss and tell, that information could only have come from you." He throws me another look of utter disgust. "Did you get some sort of kick out of telling everyone you're screwing the new CEO, Emma? Does it give you some sort of twisted power trip?"

"I didn't tell everyone!" I retort, outraged, "I told one person! My best friend! Oh my God." I trail off as it hits me, "Megs must have let it slip – someone at Carter & Boyd must have found out, and they sent her here to try and secure your contract."

"Megs?" he asks, forgetting to look terrifying for a second, "you mean Megan Harris?"

"The girl you just met with, yes."

"She's your best friend?"

"Yes. Well, she was. She worked with me at Focus for four years, until just a few weeks ago. Why?"

His expression is unreadable. "Some friends you have, Emma. Megan's the one who called me in the first place."

IT ALL COMES CRASHING down around me, too fast for me to process, and I collapse onto the white sofa. Greg only arrived back on Tuesday and Megan had called him on Wednesday morning. She hadn't wasted any time. The shock of my best friend's betrayal is mind-numbing, but through my confusion, something else dawns on me.

"Is that why you rescheduled?" I ask, glancing up at him hollowly. "Is that why you didn't call?"

"I prefer not to be used to further someone's career, Emma," he replies coldly, "no matter how pleasurable the experience may be."

"I didn't use you, you asshole! I confided in a friend – someone I trusted." My righteous indignation takes him aback. "Megan is – was – my only confidant. There must be some mistake. She wouldn't do this to me."

"There's no mistake." His tone is softer now, but only marginally.

I shake my head, trying to make sense of it all. "Megan wouldn't throw away our friendship for the sake of one account."

"It's a big account," he points out.

"It doesn't matter. She wouldn't do this. Not to me... Oh, God." I drop my head into my hands.

"What?"

"Jack," I groan, mumbling into my palms. I feel the sofa dip under his weight as he takes a seat beside me. I turn my head to peer at him. He deserves an explanation. "Megan and Jack were having an affair," I sigh, knowing that this admission could very well cost me my job. "Jack ended it and fired Megan, but not before he found her a position at Carter & Boyd. Megan swore she was going to destroy him, but I didn't think she'd actually go through with it."

"Let me get this straight," he says, sounding dubious. "Megan did all of this just to get back at Jack, even if it meant ruining your reputation?"

An ugly black rage rears in my chest. "Apparently."

"So, you didn't believe that sleeping with me would secure my business?"

"I hate to break it to you, but last week I didn't give a damn about your business," I retort. "I was more concerned about when I would see you again."

He takes time to process this, and I drop my head back into my hands. I feel ill. I still can't believe that Megan would do this to me – that she would turn on me so viciously. I know she's been upset about Jack, and taking away our biggest account would hurt him, but it hurts me far more.

"I can't believe she'd stoop this low," I mutter, reaching automatically for the coffee on the table before me.

Greg doesn't say a word. He just sits there, staring at me as if trying to figure out if I'm telling the truth. I set my cup down and get to my feet.

"I'm going to talk to her."

He stands too. "You're not going anywhere until we've figured this out."

"You figure it out," I snap. "You believed that I was capable of this, that I would stoop so low. You obviously don't know me at all, and I'm not about to try to convince you otherwise."

"How was I to know your opposition is your best friend?" he counters.

"You could have asked me! You could have talked to me instead of cutting me off and making a fool of me in front of my boss. But instead, you immediately jumped to the worst possible conclusion. Get out of my way," I add, trying to shove past him.

"No," he grabs my arms and pushes me back. "We're going to talk about this."

"Screw you."

That stops him in his tracks, and a blaze of righteous anger crosses his face.

"You walk out of that door, and I will give this contract to Carter & Boyd."

"You're threatening me now?" His silence speaks volumes. My eyes widen, incredulously. "You know what, Greg," I say, snatching up my bag. "You can go to hell." I stride toward the doors and don't look back.

I HEAD STRAIGHT for Megan's apartment. She won't be home yet, but I'll wait all night if I have to. I'm not leaving without answers. During the short cab ride over, I make two calls. The first is to Jack, explaining I will only be in tomorrow and we can debrief then, and one to my parents to say I might be a little late fetching Ally. Unsurprisingly, when I arrive at Megan's, I find that my key no longer works. She must have changed the locks. I settle down on the carpet outside her apartment to wait.

Megan gets home just before six, and I scramble to my feet as she gets out of the elevator.

I don't even bother hiding my anger. "How could you, Megan?"

"How could I what?" she replies coolly.

"You're going to destroy my career!"

"No, I'm going to destroy Jack's," she corrects.

"If I lose Nanosec I'm going to be out on my ass!"

"Carter & Boyd will take you on," she justifies. "You know the Nanosec account – they'll need you." She's so calm, so carelessly unapologetic it feels like a punch to the gut.

"You betrayed me! How could you use what I told you in confidence against me? All that time you and Jack were carrying on, and I never told a soul."

She shrugs. "Maybe you should have." Then she notices the tears welling in my eyes, and she heaves a sigh. "He's only a client, Em. You said yourself you're not even sure you guys are a thing. Besides, from what I saw on Saturday night, you've clearly moved on."

"Oh my God, are you for real? That was nothing, I told you that! Oliver and I are just friends."

"You seem to have a lot of those," she sneers.

"Not as many as I thought," I reply pointedly.

"Look, Emma, it's not personal. I have a job to do and targets to meet, and Nanosec will go a long way to meeting those targets. I still have to prove myself at C&B, it's not like Focus."

I gape at her. "Not personal? You're my *best* friend! You're trying to steal my biggest client, and worse, you used my private affairs to do it! How is that not personal?"

"Firstly, I'm not trying." She allows herself a small smile. "I'm ninety-nine percent certain that Nanosec will be signing with Carter & Boyd in the next quarter. Secondly, once you've calmed down, you'll realize that I've done you a favor."

"A favor?"

"Yes. Jack's a dick, Emma. Focus is going to fall. You're better off deserting the ship before it's sunk."

"You're insane. This isn't a movie, this is my life we're talking about. My job, my reputation!"

She pulls a face. "You're just pissed that after all these years of living in your shadow I'm finally going to be the hottest property in advertising."

I open my mouth but nothing comes out, because this accusation is so absurd, I have no words to respond. I have never seen Megs as my competition, we've always worked as a team. Apparently, she doesn't share this view. I wonder if she ever did. I never suspected the extent of her professional jealousy. Yes, I am better at my job than she is, but that's only because I work harder. Megan is lazy by nature and does the bare minimum.

"Don't you find it ironic," I sneer eventually, losing my fragile grip on my temper, "that the very thing you've accused me of is the one thing that ensured you kept your job for the past four years?"

"What?" she snaps.

"Well, if you hadn't been screwing the boss, you probably would've been fired years ago," I smile spitefully. Tossing my useless key at her, I turn on my heel.

"You are going to fall very far, princess," she calls at my retreating figure. "I'm going to take every single client you have left – Nanosec is just the beginning."

"Do your worst, Megan," I scoff, barely flinching as her apartment door slams violently behind me.

By the time I've settled Alyssa into bed and opened an expensive bottle of red wine, my black rage has settled into a dull, vengeful anger. There is no point mourning the end of a friendship that obviously meant nothing to Megan, and I am nothing if not fiercely competitive in business. Paging through my customer files, deliberately avoiding Nanosec's, I barely notice the doorbell ringing. Glancing at my watch, a sickening dread settles in the pit of my stomach. It's after ten, and there's only one person I know who would come around this late.

PEERING THROUGH THE PEEPHOLE, I am so relieved that it is not a drunken Max on the other side that I open the door.

"Greg! What are you doing here?"

"You left."

I raise my chin defiantly, recalling his ultimatum. "Yes. I left."

He has the good grace to lower his eyes first. "I shouldn't have threatened to give Carter and Boyd the account."

"It was a dick move," I concede.

"I know."

I cross my arms over my chest and lean against the door frame until he finally realizes he's not done.

"I'm sorry."

"Good."

"You understand that this isn't entirely my fault," he muses. I get the sense that he's used to getting his own way and isn't quite sure how to handle this situation.

"I know."

His blue eyes crinkle at the corners. "You're really not going to make this easy for me, are you?"

"It's been a long day."

"Did you speak to Megan?"

"I did. I think it's safe to say that friendship is over."

"Are you okay?" I blink up at him, surprised at the genuine concern in his voice. I've been so angry, it hasn't even occurred to me that I've lost my best friend.

"I will be."

He nods, slow and thoughtful.

"I should get to bed," I say, glancing at my watch.

"If you're up to it, I'd like to take you to dinner tomorrow night."

I arch my brow. "Really. And why would you possibly want to do that?"

"Because I've been a prize prick and I'd like to make it up to you?" I can't help but chuckle. "Seriously," he continues, more somber, "I'm sorry. I'd really like a second chance to prove it."

"I need to spend some time with Ally tomorrow," I say, "but Wednesday could work."

The smile he gives me is dazzling. "I'll pick you up at eight."

"No." I'm not letting him off that easy.

"No?"

"I'll make my own way and meet you there. Just let me know where."

He gives me an arch look. "Are you always this stubborn?"

I start to close the door, not giving him an answer. "Text me the address," I say, before I close it completely.

I watch him through the keyhole. A small smile plays about his lips and he shakes his head, as if he can't quite figure out what just happened, before he turns away and strides back down the path to his car.

"EMMA!" Jack snaps the second I exit the elevator the following morning. "What the hell is going on? I tried to call you a dozen times yesterday!"

"I know, I'm sorry, Jack. I did tell Chloe to let you know I wouldn't be coming back in and that I'd brief you this morning."

He's not appeased. "She told me. I don't appreciate being kept in the dark."

"I know," I echo. "But I promise it was necessary. I had to do some major damage control." That stops him in his tracks.

"Why was Megan at Nanosec? You told me this account was in the bag."

I see Oliver's head appear in the doorway behind him, but he quickly retreats, and I focus on Jack. I've never seen him this wound up.

"It is," I soothe. "That's why I needed time. Megan tried to outplay us – she's pissed – at you actually, and she did her best to pull the account away, but she failed. Nanosec is secure."

"How sure are you?"

"Ninety-nine percent sure."

He deliberates this for a second and then runs his hands through his hair, his relief palpable.

"Why would Megan do that?"

"Why do you think? You broke her heart, Jack. She wants revenge."

"She's not that petty."

I give a scornful laugh. "Apparently, neither of us knows her as well as we thought we did. And you should know, it won't end with Nanosec. She's going after all of our accounts."

Jack opens his mouth to question me and then notices one of the other executives, lurking in his open doorway. "Into my office," Jack murmurs. I follow him inside, and he shuts the door behind us. "Explain."

I collapse onto the black leather chair opposite his desk. "Megan tried to use something I'd told her in confidence against me. She went behind my back and tried to get Nanosec to jump ship. And before you ask, no, I'm not going to tell you what it was."

"I wasn't going to ask."

"Good."

"Why would she do that? I get that she's mad at me, but why would she do that to you?"

"I have no idea." I don't mention Megan's comment that I should join Carter & Boyd. It might just send Jack over the edge, and besides, I could never work in the same company as her again. Not now, not after this. "Megan is not who I thought she was."

"I can't believe she would do something like this."

"Believe it, Jack. Hell hath no fury like a woman scorned."

He cringes. "For what it's worth, I'm sorry that you got dragged into all of this."

"Me too."

"You did a good job yesterday." It's high praise, coming from Jack.

"I did. Nice of you to notice."

He lets my sarcasm slide. "You're sure the account is secure?"

"I said so didn't I?"

"You said you were ninety-nine percent sure."

"So?"

"Be a hundred percent sure. Both our asses depend on it."

THE SECOND I'm back in my office, Oliver ducks inside, emitting a low whistle.

"What was that about?"

"You wouldn't believe me if I told you." Being Oliver, he doesn't press me, but I find myself telling him most of it anyway – how Megan betrayed me and tried to steal Nanosec's account from right under my nose. Oliver is righteously outraged on my behalf, but he doesn't look as surprised as I expect him to be and I say as much.

"Yeah, well, she didn't strike me as being a very good friend," he admits.

"Why do you say that?"

His cheeks redden. "She, um, well, she propositioned me on Saturday night when I came out of the men's room."

"Oh God, what did she say?" Megan had thrown herself at Oliver most of Saturday night, but I wasn't aware she'd voiced her intentions.

"It doesn't matter." The fact that he doesn't want to tell me is a clear indication that whatever Megan said to him wasn't complimentary as far as I am concerned.

"What did she say?" I repeat, locking gazes with him.

"She might have mentioned that I should take her home because she wasn't as prim and proper as you were, and that she would do things to me that you could only," he raises his hands and puts air quotes around the rest, "dream about."

"She didn't!"

"She did!" He is half-laughing, half-disgusted. "It scared the shit out of me!"

"Well, it's hardly an insult."

"Agreed. It was more that she felt she needed to make the comparative, you know. As if it was some competition between the two of you. Anyway, in my opinion, friends don't do that."

"No, they don't," I agree. "Which is why I'm so happy that I found a new and improved bestie to take her place."

"You and Jack getting cozy?" he teases, and I throw a pad of Post-Its at him.

He catches them lazily. "Any exciting plans this week?"

"I have a date," I admit.

"A date?" he grins without a trace of awkwardness. "How exciting. Who's the lucky man?"

I don't want anyone to know about Greg yet. I'm pretty sure Jack wouldn't like it. Not that he has any say in my personal life, but with everything that's happened with Megan and Nanosec, it'll raise a red flag. "Just a guy," I tell Oliver.

He gets to his feet and walks toward the door. "Well, have fun," he teases, eyes sparkling with ill-concealed mirth.

"I will," I call back, smiling to myself.

Alyssa and I head for the movies right after work. It's a school night so we catch the early show. She's been withdrawn since last weekend when I had to fetch her from Max's, and he hadn't bothered to show up for his visit this past Saturday. After the movie, I treat her to ice-cream, and she slowly comes out of her shell.

"I miss daddy," she admits guiltily.

"Of course you do, angel. It's okay to miss him," I add, trying to reassure her. "But daddy's going to come and see you on Sunday." As I say it, I vow to make it happen whether Max likes it or not. "We can go to the park, if you like?"

She brightens instantly. "All of us?"

"All of us," I promise. She nods her head in excitement at the very thought, and I suppress a sigh. All I ever wanted for Alyssa was for her to grow up in a safe, stable environment. To feel loved and adored by her parents and never experience even a token of what I felt as a child. But Max screwed that all up, and yet I'm the one who has to deal with the consequences.

She falls asleep on the drive home with chocolate ice-cream all over her face. Not wanting to wake her, I wipe her down with a warm cloth and tuck her into bed.

Ten minutes later, armed with a scalding cup of tea, I dial Max's number.

"Hello?" he answers immediately.

"Hi. I'm sorry to call so late, we just got back from the movies."

"That's okay. What did you guys go see?" To my surprise, he sounds completely sober. He doesn't bring up the missed visit, and I find myself not wanting to either.

"The new Dumbo."

He laughs. "Was it any better than the old one?"

"Not particularly."

"Did Ally enjoy herself?"

"She had ice-cream. Need I say more?"

I hate to ruin this fragile peace, but I have to bring it up for Ally's sake. "You missed your visit on Saturday," I say. I hear him exhale a shuddery breath. "Max?"

"I'm sorry. I..." he trails off, and I bite my lip to stop from filling the silence. "I have a lot to tell you," he says eventually. "But I'd rather do it in person."

"Okay," I draw out the word. "Should I be worried?"

"No. Can I come over this Saturday?"

"Actually, that's why I was calling. Ally wants to go to the park. I thought maybe we could have a picnic." I cringe, waiting for him to snap, to insist that I'm not only insisting on supervised visits, but now dictating what we do during those visits. To my utter astonishment, Max agrees.

"Sounds good. Can I bring anything?"

"No, I'll pack a basket. Can you meet us there at ten? The one on the corner of Madison and Sixth."

"Sure. I'll see you then."

"See you then." I hang up, not quite sure what just happened. It feels oddly surreal. I've never denied that when Max is sober, he is one of the nicest people I know. Buried within the depths of his alcoholism is the man I fell in love with – the man I was prepared to spend the rest of my life with. It is nothing short of tragic that his disease was stronger than his love for his family, but I have come to accept that's exactly what it is – a disease. Max is ill, and there is nothing anybody can do to heal him. I can only hope that one day he finds the strength and the courage to heal himself.

THE FOLLOWING EVENING, I have the house to myself. Alyssa is sleeping at my parents. My dad fetched her straight from school, and he'll drop her off in the morning, so I'm officially off duty for twenty-four hours. I shave my legs, paint my toenails, and even give myself a mini-facial, which includes a bentonite clay mask that makes me look like something out of a horror movie. When I wash it off, I see no visible difference. Go figure.

I pull the tag off the dress I bought during my lunch break. It's coral, high at the neck and plunging at the back. The soft fabric clings to my body in all the right places. I'm meeting Greg at eight, but with so much time on my hands, I arrive early.

"Would you like me to show you to your table?" the waiter asks. I decline and opt to wait at the bar. By the time Greg arrives ten minutes later, I'm halfway through my first Martini.

"You look..." Greg trails off, his eyes roaming the entire length of my body. He doesn't finish the sentence.

"You too," I murmur shyly. His athletic frame would make anything look good, but the dark grey chinos and open-collared white shirt is the perfect balance of smart-casual.

"Have you forgiven me yet?" he asks.

"I haven't decided."

A low chuckle and his arm brushes against mine. "Should we go sit down? I'm starving."

The waiter darts forward to show us to our table. Greg pulls out my chair, leaving the poor man hovering with one arm outstretched. Greg orders a bottle of red, giving him something to do.

"I assume your daughter is safe and sound tonight, and we won't need to be paying any surprise visits to your ex?"

"She is," I nod, "she's at my folks. And Max is actually being pretty agreeable." He doesn't comment, but I can see the hard, unforgiving doubt in his blue eyes.

"I never asked about your race," I say, changing the subject. "How did you do?"

"We did well."

"We?"

"It was a team event. Eight of us participated."

"Oh, nice." I shut my mouth because I have no idea what the correct response is. I know nothing about cycling.

As if reading my thoughts, he gives me a wicked grin. "How's the swimming going?" *Oh shit.* I'd forgotten about that. I'm supposed to be a swimmer. Obviously, I haven't done any swimming lately, other than an awkward doggy paddle around my parent's pool with Alyssa on the occasional hot day.

"I did a few laps this morning at the gym," I reply airily. His gaze flickers up from the bread roll he's smearing with butter, and he raises a skeptical eyebrow.

"Which gym?"

I open my mouth and realize I have no idea where the closest gym is. In fact, I have no idea where any gym is. Greg is still staring at me, an amused expression on his face.

"Okay fine, I don't go to the gym. In fact, I don't swim – well, not the way you think. I'm more of a professional floater. The thing is, work keeps me pretty busy, and I have a four-year-old daughter who takes up every minute of my life not spent working, so I don't really do much in the way of exercise."

He hands me the roll, liberally buttered, his eyes never leaving my face.

"You think I'm a slob, don't you?"

"No. I think you're adorable."

I blush crimson at the blatant desire on his face. Then he winces.

"What?" I ask.

"Nothing," he says, but he shifts uncomfortably on his chair. I lower my gaze and comprehension dawns.

"Oh!"

"Do you have this effect on all men, or am I just powerless to your charms?"

"I think it might just be you."

"I think you don't give yourself enough credit."

Now that I know he's horny, I find I can't concentrate on anything else. A sleeping beast in my chest opens one eye and purrs.

Our conversation is interrupted by the waiter, who returns to take our order. We settle on a seafood platter for two, but the second the waiter leaves, Greg drops his napkin and moves around the table to sit beside me. His arm trails along the back of the seat, his fingers brushing the ends of my hair. It's intimate and unnerving, having him so close, but I shift so that my hip presses up against his. I meet the challenge in his gaze. Hidden by the starched table cloth, his other hand clamps over my thigh. His thumb traces a lazy circle, setting my skin on fire.

I snatch up the glass of water on the table and drink deeply.

"Is it hot in here, or is it just me?" I ask, flashing Greg a grin and trying to break the mounting tension. He doesn't respond. Instead, his forefinger joins his thumb, inching upward with every lazy circle. When his hand finally cups that most sensitive part of me, I bite my tongue to stifle the gasp of pleasure which threatens to claw its way out of my throat. This is so surreal, so primal, and reckless, but I raise my hips, returning the pressure of his hand. Greg's eyes are glittering, his pupils dilated. Beneath the skirt of my dress, my thighs open of their own accord and his fingers slip inside my pants.

By the time the waiter returns, my breathing is coming in short, sharp gasps. He gives me a strange look as he deposits an enormous tray before us, but one narrow-eyed look from Greg is all the warning he needs to make himself scarce.

The pressure building between my legs is almost at breaking point. I clamp my hand onto Greg's thigh, needing to ground myself, and my nails dig in. It takes everything in me to keep my expression neutral, to act as though this entire restaurant hasn't been reduced to the blazing heat of my very core. I reach the brink and start to topple over and, just as quickly as he started, Greg whips his hand away, abandoning his merciless assault on my body.

I exhale in a wave of despair as tiny shockwaves ripple through me, fading with every passing second.

"What are you doing?" I breathe. My head feels too heavy for my neck. At least when he speaks, he sounds just as affected as I am, his voice hoarse.

"I think it's called foreplay," he says. He picks a juicy pink prawn from the plate, his deft fingers peeling it expertly before he hands it to me. It's dripping in lemon butter.

"My cardiologist thanks you," I manage to joke before I pop it into my mouth. It's heavenly. I take a small sip of wine, wipe my fingers on my napkin and meet Greg's gaze. His eyes are dancing.

"You're trouble with a capital T," I say.

Without missing a beat, he leans forward and puts his lips on mine, his tongue sweeping mine so quickly I might have imagined it as he savors the lingering taste in my mouth. My blood sings, rushing to my head and thundering in my ears.

"Enough."

"Enough?" he asks, his brow raised in challenge. I have no doubt he'd go on all night if I let him, but quite frankly my body cannot take another second of his teasing.

I lean forward, my lips pulling up at the corners, and boldly place my hand over the front of his pants. Greg almost lurches out of his seat as his hand flies into the air.

"Cheque please," he gasps.

We don't make it home. We barely even make it to his car, before I'm tearing at his clothes. In one swift movement, he hikes my dress over my hips, which is all he can manage in the confined space. I spare a fleeting moment of gratitude for the darkly tinted windows before his mouth claims mine, and all I know is oblivion.

11

During the drive home, I keep bursting into fits of giggles. Even Greg can't keep the smile off his face, although his is far smugger, no doubt as a result of the three orgasms he coaxed out of me, despite the cramped space and an awkward pause when an elderly couple ventured too close to the window, and he'd almost castrated himself on the gearstick.

Despite it all, I'm still not satisfied.

"Ally is sleeping over at my folks tonight," I say pointedly as we turn into my street. His teeth flash in the dim light of the car.

"Had this all planned, did you?"

"Believe me, what happened tonight wasn't premeditated."

He pulls up outside my house and rounds the car to open my door, then retrieves a small black overnight bag from the trunk.

"Who's presumptuous now?" I tease, but my heart stutters in anticipation. He holds my hand as we walk up the path, and it's so easy, so comfortable. Once inside, I head straight for my room and into the en suite to turn on the shower. I stick my head out of the door and give him a lingering look. "You coming?"

He doesn't need to be asked twice.

Later, we lie on sheets still damp from our after-shower tussle. I nestle in the crook of Greg's shoulder while his fingers trail over my arm. My stomach growls, and we both laugh, thinking of the wasted seafood platter.

"I have my son next weekend," Greg says after a time. "How about we go bike riding? Alyssa would love it." I blink in the dark. I really, really like him, but I balk at the thought of spending a whole day with him and his son so soon. I don't want Alyssa meeting anyone I date until I'm sure that they are going to become a part of my life.

"She doesn't really know how to ride a bike," I say, cringing at the flimsy excuse. "She still has training wheels."

"Even better, we can teach her."

"She's only four."

"Jesse's been riding without them since he was three. She'll pick it up in no time, I promise."

"I just don't think..."

"That we should meet each other's kids?" he finishes my sentence.

"Well, yeah."

"We don't need to make a big deal out of it. We're just friends, spending the day together. Our kids don't need to know any more than that. Unless you don't trust yourself to keep your hands off me, which would be perfectly understandable." His grin is infectious.

"It sounds fun," I concede, throwing caution to the wind. "But we'll have to make it Sunday. Saturday is Max's day with Ally."

"Sunday is perfect." My stomach rumbles again, and Greg gets to his feet. He rummages in the black bag and pulls out a pair of sleeping shorts, which he pulls on before offering me his hand. I eye it, bemused. "I'm going to make you a sandwich," he says, by way of explanation. "There's no way I'm going to get any sleep with that noise."

I sit at the kitchen table while he smears peanut butter on two slices of bread. He slaps them together and cuts four perfect triangles before pushing the plate toward me.

"You're not even going to cut off my crusts?" I tease.

"Eat your crusts, they're good for you."

I take a bite while he fetches the milk from the fridge and pours me a generous glass. Only once he's taken the seat opposite me do I stop eating. This is easily one of the best evenings I've spent in a long time. Greg is confident, cocky, and surprisingly funny for someone who is so ruthless in business.

"How are you single?" I blurt out. He doesn't seem surprised by the question.

"Work takes up a lot of my time."

"I don't buy that. All men say that, but it doesn't stop them taking care of their physical needs."

He shrugs. "You didn't ask about my physical needs. You asked why I was single."

"Oh," I say. I wish hadn't asked.

"I'm not promiscuous," he says, his eyes holding mine, "but I certainly haven't been celibate since the separation."

"And this?" I ask, waving a sandwich triangle between us. "Is this something you might have time for?"

He gives me an arch look. "Are you asking me if we're dating?" I feel the heat rise in my cheeks, but I stand my ground.

"I'm asking if this is just a physical needs arrangement, or if it's something more."

His blue eyes soften. "It's definitely something more."

"I'm honored." I grin. "What with you being so busy and all."

"What about you? Have you dated much since your divorce?"

"No. And before you ask, I haven't really taken care of my physical need either."

"Anytime you need help in that department, I'd be happy to oblige."

"How generous of you."

He spreads his arms. "What can I say? I'm a generous guy."

"And so humble."

He laughs at that and then stands to take my empty plate to the sink.

"We should get some sleep. I have an early start."

"Have you had time to review my proposal?"

"Yes, actually. There are a few things I'd like to change, but all in all, it's sound."

My professional pride protests. "What changes?"

"Why don't you swing by my office tomorrow afternoon and we can go through it."

"Okay, sure." We walk down the hall, and something else occurs to me. "Have you heard from Megan at all?"

"Yes, actually. She called me this morning to set up a follow-up appointment."

I feel my hackles rise as we climb into bed. "What did you tell her?"

"I told her to come see me on Monday."

"What? Why?"

He pulls my head onto his chest. "So that I can tell her in person that Nanosec will not now, or ever, have any interest in doing business with Carter & Boyd," he replies, eerily calm.

"Why didn't you just tell her over the phone?"

"Because I want to tell her in front of her boss. I asked that she bring him along."

"What?"

"Megan crossed a line. He needs to know what kind of employee he's brought into his company."

"But she'll be fired! You can't do that!" This is yet another glimpse into the fact that below all his charm lurks a ruthless businessman.

"I can, and I will," Greg counters. "Nobody manipulates me, Emma. Megan Harris's career in advertising is over."

It is the first time I become aware that he is capable of cruelty. His ego, however, in no way diminishes his sex appeal. If anything, it only makes him that much more attractive. Max was weak, which is why he couldn't fight his addiction. It's also no less than Megan deserves. Setting aside how she treated me, the way she conducted herself was appalling and utterly unprofessional. And yet, as angry as I am with her, I don't want her to lose her job.

"I don't think you should do it," I murmur quietly.

"Emma, this isn't personal, and it has nothing to do with me and you. I'm not that petty. Megan's actions were unprofessional, and she deserves to be disciplined."

"I guess."

"But?" he can sense that I am biting my tongue.

"It just seems a bit cruel."

"I can be cruel," he says matter-of-factly and without the slightest bit of contrition. "Does that bother you?"

"I don't know," I admit.

He sighs and raises himself onto his elbow, head propped in his hand. "Look, Emma, I like you. A lot, if I'm being honest. But this is how I do things. I didn't get to where I am by being nice, so unless you can give me a very good reason why I shouldn't bring Megan's misdemeanors to light, I'm not changing my mind."

12

Come Saturday, Ally is in one of her rare, overly-excited moods.

"Calm down!" I say, for what feels like the twentieth time, as we pull into the parking lot. The sound of children playing reaches me instantly. Ignoring me completely, Ally opens her door and leaps down from her seat, making a beeline for the playground.

"Alyssa!" I scream in horror, as a white station wagon pulls into the lot. Ally streaks directly toward its approaching path. She either doesn't hear me, or she is too buoyed up to listen, and I am too far away to do anything about it, but I dart forward anyway, my heart in my throat.

A strong pair of arms grab her at the last minute and pull her out of the path of the oncoming car. My legs buckle in relief.

"Max!" I gasp as I reach them, clutching my chest. "Oh, thank God." Max holds an unsuspecting Alyssa tightly, his mouth a hard, grim line.

"How could you let her run across the lot on her own?" he thunders angrily.

"I didn't! She ran off!" I place my hand on her shoulder, desperate to reassure myself that she's okay.

"That's not good enough, Em! That car could have hit her!"

"I know!" Tears prick at my eyelids. Being taken to task by the worst parent in the world is humiliating and grossly unfair, but he's right. "I'll put the child-locks on," I promise, trying to diffuse the situation. "You take her to the playground, I'll fetch our stuff." He turns on his heel without another word, and I head back to the car to retrieve our bags, my heart still thudding violently in my chest.

Our morning is not off to a great start, but soon Alyssa's infectious delight perks both Max and I up.

"How are things at work?" he asks placatingly after about an hour of disapproving silence.

"Good." I wave at Ally on the swings, "Megan has left. She's gone over to Carter & Boyd."

"Isn't Carter & Boyd your opposition? That's got to be tough on the friendship," he whistles sympathetically.

"To say the least. We're not really friends anymore."

"You didn't let work come between you, did you?"

"No," I shake my head. "I have no problem with professional rivalry. She just... well, let's just say she betrayed me in a very dirty, underhanded way."

"I'm sorry to hear that," he says, sounding as though he means it.

"Thanks."

Max wanders off to play with Ally, and I lie back on the blue-and-white checked blanket, closing my eyes and letting the sun warm my skin. The sound of laughter and a healthy dose of vitamin D is far better than any therapy, I think lazily. Dozing lightly between sleep and wakefulness, I give a humph of surprise when Alyssa jumps onto my belly a short while later, driving all the air from my lungs.

"Daddy's getting us ice-cream," she announces, her cheeks flushed with excitement. A moment later Max hands me a lolly – raspberry, my favorite.

"You know me too well," I remark drily, without really thinking.

In times like these, it's easy to forget the horror of our divorce and the events leading up to it.

"Better than you know yourself." It was his standard response when we were together, and the familiar teasing makes me feel both nostalgic and irritated.

After we've packed up, Max walks us to the car. With Alyssa strapped safely in her seat, he makes a point of checking that the child-lock is on before closing her door and turning to face me.

"Look, Emma, about the court order."

"Please," I hold up my hand to stop him, "let's not get into this now. I'm not trying to hurt you—"

"I know that," he cuts me off. "I just wanted to say that I'm sorry. I'm disgusted with myself for how I acted that night – for how I behaved. I don't want to lose her..." he trails off as he gazes through the window. Alyssa is smiling up at us, oblivious to our tense conversation. "Anyway, I wanted you to be the first to know that I've joined A.A."

It takes me a full minute for the words to register, and when they do, the impact they have is remarkable.

"Really?" I feel like I might burst into tears.

"Really," he nods. "I don't want to end up being a deadbeat dad with nothing to show for my life. I've already ruined the best thing I ever had."

"Max, that's wonderful. I'm so proud of you." Stepping forward, I hug him properly for the first time in years. His arms come around me naturally, and another wave of nostalgia washes over me. "If there is anything I can do to help, just let me know."

"Actually," he releases me and looks slightly sheepish, "there's a meeting in a few weeks. They want us to bring someone along – someone directly affected by our drinking. I think it's part of the healing process and taking responsibility for the damage we've caused."

"I'm there," I say without hesitation. "Just let me know when and where, and I'm there." I smile up at him, seeing him in a new light.

There is no possibility that Max and I will ever reconcile, but this could mean so much for his relationship with our daughter. And if he stops drinking, I might be able to trust him again. I could revoke the court order, and everything could go back to the way it was.

"Thanks, Em," he murmurs.

"You're very welcome." I give him a quick hug and climb into the driver's seat. Max waves as we pull out of the lot.

13

"I'm five minutes away," Greg says when I answer his call the following morning.

"We're almost ready," I say, a smile in my voice. I've been up since dawn, packing a picnic.

Exactly five minutes later Greg pulls up to my curb in a flashy black SUV. I'm already locking the front door as he gets out to greet us. He doesn't try to kiss my cheek as he usually does, keeping to his word in front of Alyssa.

I smile up at him, grateful that she can't read my expression. "Where's your car?"

"This is my car. I have more than one," he admits sheepishly, catching sight of my arch look. "And in my defense, the bikes won't fit in the Beemer."

He loads Alyssa's bicycle in the back and I strap her in beside a cherubic-looking little boy with Greg's green eyes and dimples he could only have inherited from his mother.

"You must be Jesse," I say, smiling at him. He doesn't reply, but the dimples deepen shyly.

"He sure is," Greg announces, settling into the driver's seat and swiveling to face his son. "Jess, this is my friend Emma who I was telling you about, and that's Alyssa, her daughter." Jesse and Ally give each other an appraising once-over before turning back to face us.

"Maybe we should just get going," I tell Greg, trying not to laugh.

The park he takes us to is surrounded by a broad bicycle track which means that I'm able to lay down a blanket and set up our picnic without ever losing sight of Alyssa. I settle down to watch as she pedals furiously after Jesse, who, by the look of it, has been riding since birth.

"We should get those training wheels off," Greg tells me after a time.

I frown. "I don't know. If she falls, she might lose all her confidence."

"And if she doesn't, she'll gain a whole lot more," he counters.

I'm still not convinced. "Let me ask her."

Ally is hesitant but willing to try. Within minutes, Greg has the trainers off, and I find myself jogging alongside her as she wobbles on the bike. Greg joins me on the second lap, a secretive smile plastered on his handsome face.

"Don't," I warn, conscious of my jiggling backside and the fact that my bra is far more sexy than supportive.

"I wasn't going to say anything," he lies, and then, lowering his voice so Alyssa won't hear, "let her go, she's got it."

Slowly, I ease my firm grip on Ally's seat. I jog beside her for at least fifteen meters before she wobbles, and I grab hold of her again. "Well done!" I yell, triumphantly, "you were riding all by yourself!"

"Don't let go, mommy!" she shrieks, but I can hear the euphoria beneath her fear. As soon as she's stable, I let go again. After four more laps, I'm drenched in perspiration and gasping for breath, but Alyssa is riding on her own.

"Mommy needs a break," I pant, conscious of Greg jogging along beside me, barely breaking a sweat.

"Here, let me take over," he offers. Gratefully, I accept and head back to the picnic blanket.

Five minutes later, Greg joins me, while Ally and Jesse race around the track. Ally is nowhere near as fast as Jesse, but that doesn't stop her from trying her best to catch up with him.

"I can't believe she's riding on her own," I breathe in awe.

"She's a fast learner," Greg concedes, with the smug charm of a man who's been proved right.

"Thanks for doing this. It's nice to have a man around who knows how to handle this kind of thing."

"This kind of thing, as in cardio?" he teases.

I throw a grape at him. He catches it easily and pops it in his mouth. "You should come out with me one day – on the bikes, I mean. I think you'd enjoy it."

"Hmm-mmm," I mumble, non-committal. "I'll think about it."

When they drop us off around midday, Greg and Jesse come inside. The kids disappear into Alyssa's bedroom and soon the familiar sound of games on her iPad float down the hall. Greg steps up behind me as I fill two glasses with ice, his hard body pressed up against mine. I ignore him and set about making two cups, while my heart flip-flops in my chest. When his hand steals up my shorts, encountering bare thigh, I almost slosh soda all over the counter.

"It sounds like they'll be occupied for a while," Greg croons in my ear, his voice low and inviting as his fingers creep northward. I lean back into him, feeling the hard nudge of him against my backside, and my head droops back onto his shoulder. The ice is melted by the time we're done.

"You are incorrigible," I tell him later when we settle onto the sofa, drinks in hand.

He gives me a devilish grin. "I didn't hear you complaining, although I did hear a few noises I wouldn't mind hearing again."

"You're making me blush."

"I should hope so." He sets his glass down. "When do I get to see you alone again, so we can finish what we started?"

. . .

THE PROBLEM with dating when you have small children and are trying to keep it secret, I realize as the weeks go by, is that you never feel fully satisfied. Stolen moments, fast and furious sex, fully-clothed, all add to the thrill of it, but I'm starting to look forward to having our relationship out in the open. I do love the long, lazy nights on the rare occasion we get the house to ourselves. Greg is insatiable, and an expert lover. I'm surprised I'm not bow-legged every time he leaves. I've spent a few evenings at his place, too, although it took me a few visits before I could get used to the opulence of it. "You live like a Kardashian," I'd told him. He'd laughed and admitted he'd always had a thing for Kourtney.

I don't see or hear from Megan for almost three months, so my gasp of astonishment, when she barges into my office one Thursday morning, is completely genuine. Between Alyssa, work, and my relationship with Greg, I've been too busy to even think about her. I'd heard through Greg that she'd received a warning once her boss had heard about her unprofessional conduct, but as far as I knew, she was still working at Carter and Boyd.

"What are you doing here?" I demand. Unruffled, she drapes herself over the visitor's chair opposite my desk and examines her fingernails.

"Word has it you have your eye on the Greaves account," she announces. "I'm here to tell you not to waste your time."

Greaves Dawson is an international conglomerate which manufactures a range of health foods and spends millions of dollars a year on advertising. They're also one of Carter & Boyd's biggest accounts.

"They reached out," I tell Megan, feeling my hackles rise. It's true – only last week I'd got the call from their head of marketing, calling for a meeting.

"Bullshit!" Megan hisses, losing some of her sass.

I shrug. "I guess they're not happy with how Carter & Boyd are handling their portfolio."

"You mean how *I'm* handling it."

"Your words, not mine," I counter.

"Is that how you're going to play this now, Emma? Poaching clients?"

"Like I said, they approached me. And in case you've forgotten, Megan, you started this by going after Nanosec."

She jumps on the name like a cat. "Speaking of Nanosec. I believe Greg Daniels is quite close with Greaves' head of marketing. Joanna, I think her name is." She waits for a response, but I remain silent, refusing to be baited. "*Very* close, if my sources are correct."

"Get out."

"Are you still seeing him?"

"That's none of your business."

"Oh," she feigns sympathy, "you are. Poor thing. Well, I guess so long as the work's coming in, there's no need not to share. Who knows, maybe he'll get his new friend to sign you on when our contract expires."

I get to my feet. "I told you to leave. I won't ask again." For a second, her face falls, and I catch a glimpse of the old Megan, but it's gone before I can blink. "What happened to you?" I ask before I can help myself. "We were friends. Why are you doing this?"

She gives me a pitiful look. "We were never friends, Emma. You were a means to an end – an alibi, nothing more."

I nod. "Well, then I guess there's nothing more to say."

I SHOULD HAVE KNOWN she wasn't here for me. The second Megan steps into the hall, her eyes cut to Jack's office.

"Don't even think about it," I begin, but it's too late. His door opens and Jack steps out into the hall. It takes him three seconds to notice Megan's presence. Megan flashes him a smile and then she swivels on her inch-high heels and sashays toward the elevator.

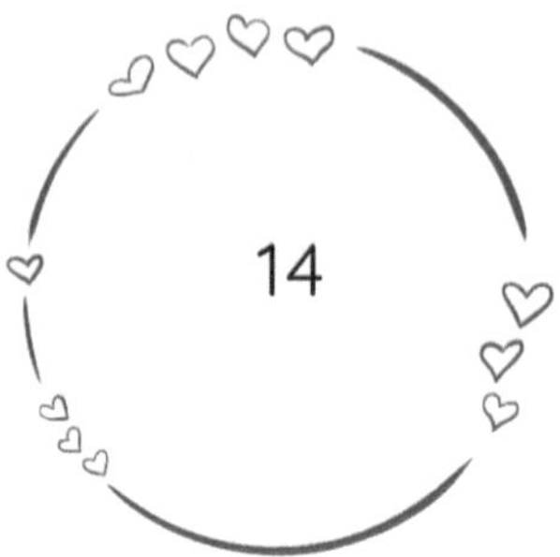

"I can't believe she barged into your office like that," Oliver says. We're in my car, I'm driving, and I've been catching him up with what's happened. Oliver was away on conference this past week, so he missed the entire episode. I'd missed him. Over the past few months, he has cemented himself well and truly as my person at Focus – my work-husband, as Greg likes to call him. I tell him everything, although I omit the details about Jack and Megan. That's not my secret to tell.

"She was so brazen," I tell him, indicating left. "She just walked in as if she owned the place."

"How did the meeting with Greaves go?"

I sigh. "Well. Very well, actually."

"And yet you don't sound happy about it?"

"I'm ninety-nine percent certain they're jumping ship."

"You know this is a good thing, right? Greaves are almost as big as Nanosec."

"I know. I'm just not looking forward to Megan's reaction."

He gazes out of the window, watching suburbia fall away. "Do you think she's mentally stable?"

I frown. Three months ago I would've laughed at the question, but now I'm not so sure. Oliver seems to sense my distress because he changes the subject.

"How're things with Max?"

That brings a genuine smile to my face. "He's doing so well. Ally is with him today, I'm picking her up later."

Max had been true to his word. He recently celebrated his ninetieth day of sobriety. I went with him to the meeting. I even brought a cake.

"That's good. I'm glad he's getting his shit together."

I glance across at him. "You don't sound so sure."

"I just don't think you should get your hopes up. It's a lifelong struggle."

"I know. Thanks for that, Debbie Downer."

We pull onto the dirt road that leads to the beginning of the cycle trail.

"I can't believe you're making me do this," Oliver grumbles as we emerge from his car.

"Oh, come on, it'll be fun. And just think of the women you might meet."

"I've sworn off women, remember." It had taken weeks before Simone had finally stopped harassing him.

"Until the next crazy lady who bats her eyelashes at you," I tease. "Besides, you're owning those pants." The cycling tights he's wearing leave nothing to the imagination.

"You made it!" Greg's voice reaches us as soon as I switch off the engine, and I turn to see him striding over, fully kitted out in tights, form-fitting shirt, and cycling shoes. Only Greg could make that ridiculous helmet look sexy, I think, my stomach flip-flopping at the sight of him. We've been dating for months, and yet he still has this effect on me. I still haven't asked him about the infamous Joanna. We haven't spent any time alone since Megan mentioned her, but with Ally sleeping out we have the house to ourselves this evening. I vow to bring it up later. Oliver averts his eyes as Greg kisses me hello. I can see my reflection in his sunglasses.

"We did," I reply, feigning a confidence I don't feel.

"Well, saddle up, we're leaving in five." Greg squeezes my ass before making his way back to a small group nearby. I pout as I realize the group is predominantly made up of women, who have eyes only for him.

"When are you just going to come clean and admit you'd rather be on the sofa watching tv?" Oliver asks.

"I wouldn't!" I argue, and then, seeing the knowing smirk on his face, I relent. "Okay, I so would, but he loves it. I'm being *supportive*."

"You're being a dork. Why don't we just leave now and save ourselves the hassle?"

"We are doing this, Mr. James. Now saddle up – you heard the man."

DESPITE MY BRAVADO, I am terrified. I finally bowed to Greg's subliminal pressure and started cycling a month ago, but it is completely out of my comfort zone. I also dragged an unwilling Oliver into my mess, needing someone who feels the same to sympathize with me. Watching the lady cyclists fawning over my boyfriend wasn't really my idea of fun, but I never let that on to Greg. Only Oliver knows how I truly feel about it

"Do you really think I'm being naïve about Max?" I ask him as we don our helmets.

"There's nothing wrong with giving him the benefit of the doubt. I just don't want you to be disappointed if it doesn't work out."

"He's really trying. And it's important for Alyssa to have a relationship with her dad."

Oliver is struggling with his helmet clip, and I reach forward to help him.

"That is not true. My dad was an asshole, and I turned out just fine," he quips.

"According to who?" I grin.

"You guys ready?" Greg calls, mounting his bike.

"Absolutely!" I reply brightly.

Half an hour later, my legs are burning, and my shirt is drenched in sweat as we pedal over dirt paths and tree roots. The terrain is even rougher than I expected, and my heart rate is going through the roof. Oliver and I have fallen behind, but no matter how hard I push myself, we don't seem to be catching up. Peals of laughter and muted conversation carry back to me on the wind.

"At least they're having fun," Oliver pants behind me. "I can't believe you forced me into this," he adds petulantly.

"It's good for us," I huff back.

"I'm going to have a heart attack. I'm pretty sure that's not good for me."

"Stop moaning and pedal."

We finally catch up to the others at a small, rickety wooden bridge that can only accommodate one rider at a time. I watch in trepidation as one by one, the cyclists cross over. It's not a long drop, but the bridge is narrower than anything I've had to traverse before.

"Can we go around?" Oliver asks, echoing my sentiments.

"You'll be fine," Greg reassures us. "But maybe it's better if I help you over, Em. I'll come back and take your bike over – you walk across."

I sense rather than see the smug smiles of the women cyclists.

"No, I'm fine," I snap, gritting my teeth.

"Emma."

"I said I'm fine."

He hesitates a moment but then slowly pedals onto the bridge.

"You're a stubborn ass," Oliver murmurs behind me. "And why didn't he offer to take my bike over?" I burst out laughing.

"Right," I say, once everyone else has crossed. "Let's do this."

"Let's not," Oliver grumbles, but I place my foot firmly on the pedal and push off onto the bridge.

. . .

I WAKE up to the sound of frantic voices and a ringing in my ears. Greg's face looms over me, filled with concern. When he sees my eyes open, he sags in relief.

"What happened?" I croak.

Oliver's face appears behind Greg's. "You fell on your ass," he says, not even trying to hide his smile. "Well, technically, you fell on your head."

Oh, God. I pull myself into a seated position and take in the sea of faces. "I fell?"

Greg is still tight-lipped. "You fell," he confirms. "You caught the railing on the way down and knocked yourself out."

"How's my bike?"

A tiny tug at the corner of his mouth. "Your bike is fine. Still, you shouldn't ride after that hit, you might be concussed. I've called for an emergency collection, they should be here in a few minutes."

"Okay." I'm mortified.

"You guys keep going," Greg tells the others. "We'll see you back at the start."

A chorus of disappointment rises up. "You should go," I tell him. "I can wait on my own."

"I'll wait with her," Oliver offers.

Greg isn't happy. I can tell by the set of his jaw, the way his eyes flicker from my face to the group behind me. Torn.

"Go," I repeat.

He gives Oliver a long, appraising look. "You sure?" he asks me.

I swallow down the knot of disappointment which has formed in my throat. "I'm sure."

Abruptly, he comes to a decision. "Okay. We're not far from the end, I won't be long. If you need me, call me. Joanna knows the way, she can guide the others if I need to bail."

His lips brush my temple. I blink rapidly as he gets to his feet and walks away. *Did he just say, Joanna?*

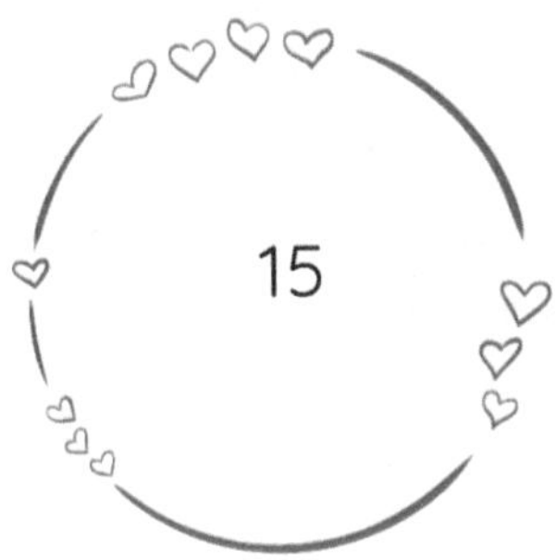

15

It's not long before we hear the rumble of the powerful 4x4 engine. Our bikes are loaded up, and Oliver and I are driven back to where we started. The medic gives me a thorough examination and concludes that I'm not concussed, but that I will have a thumping headache. I swallow down the pills he gives me and slump on the ground, pressing an ice pack to the impressive egg-shaped swelling on my forehead.

"Why so glum?" Oliver asks, taking a seat on the loamy soil beside me. He takes the ice pack and holds it for me.

"He did say, Joanna, right? I wasn't imagining it?"

"You weren't. Why, is that important?"

"Megan implied that something was going on between Greg and a woman named Joanna."

He winces. "Shit."

"Yeah."

"Do you want me to take you home?"

My head is throbbing, and I feel weepy enough that I might burst into tears. "Yes, please."

I ask the medic to let Greg know that I wasn't feeling well and decided to go home.

"You better come in, I'll call you a cab," I tell Oliver when we pull up in front of my house. There's no way I'll be able to drive him home.

"You go lie down, I can do it."

I nod gratefully and sink onto the sofa. Every time I close my eyes, my head spins. Oliver sets a cup of tea on the table before me, and I smile gratefully.

"You feeling okay?" he asks.

"No."

"If it helps, it was a spectacular fall. Really impressive. It was like you'd practiced."

I throw a cushion at him. "Do you think he'd cheat on me?"

Oliver's lips tighten. "I'd like to say no," he begins hesitantly, "but I honestly don't know. I barely know the guy, Em."

"You know him well enough," I point out, but Oliver refuses to say anything further. It's all the confirmation I need.

"Are you sure you're going to be okay? I can stay. I don't like the thought of leaving you here on your own."

"I'm fine. My pride's bruised more than anything."

"Okay, well at least me fetch Ally for you."

"Would you mind?" I smile gratefully.

"Of course not. Besides, I might even snag some of Mrs. J's shortbread while I'm there."

I laugh at that. My parents adored Oliver at first meeting, and since he demolished an entire tray of my mother's shortbread, she's constantly sending me into the office with baked goods for him."

"No doubt," I say. "Thanks, Oliver."

He leans in and kisses my cheek. He smells of sweat and soap. It's a nice smell. "I'll see you in a bit, Em," he says. Only once I hear the front door close behind him do I let the tears fall.

I'm finally dozing off when Greg erupts into the house like a tornado.

"Emma!" I can hear him calling for me the second he crosses the threshold.

"I'm in here!" I call back. He's beside me almost immediately.

"You left," he says. His voice is laced with anger and accusation.

"I'm sorry. I wasn't feeling well, and I figured it'd be easier if I just got out of the way."

His head jerks up. "Out of the way?"

"Yeah, well, there were a lot of people there, and I didn't want to be a killjoy."

"Are you being serious?" he's building up steam and I feel my own hackles rising.

"Who is Joanna?"

That throws him. "What?"

"Joanna. Who is she?"

His brow creases in confusion. "Joanna Meadon?"

"I have no idea what her last name is."

"She's a friend. She was there today – you met her."

"No, actually, I didn't. You didn't introduce me to anyone."

"Jesus, Emma, I'm sorry. There were over twenty cyclists out there today, it must have slipped my mind. I can't keep track of who knows who."

"I'm not just one of your cyclist friends! I'm your girlfriend!"

"I know that! I just don't understand where you're going with this."

My head is pounding. I take a deep breath and start again. "Megan came to see me this week. She implied that something was going on between you and a woman named Joanna."

"And you believed her?" He's incredulous.

"I'm asking you."

"Let me get this straight. Megan – a proven liar – tells you that I'm involved with someone else and you actually considered there might be some truth in it?"

"I don't know what to think. I want to trust you, but I've been burned before. I won't be naïve."

When he speaks again, his voice is so low I have to strain to hear him. "You're comparing me to Max?"

Too late, I realize my mistake. "No!" I grab his hand. "Greg, no! That's not what I meant." This is all spinning out of control, and I force myself to lower my voice. "Megan came to see me on Thursday. That was two days ago, and I haven't even mentioned anything until now. I didn't think it was true, but I had to ask."

"Okay, then, while we're on the topic, how about we talk about Oliver."

I blink in confusion. "Oliver?"

"Yes, Oliver! You told me to leave, and you chose him to stay with you. Do you have any idea how that made me feel?"

"I didn't choose him over you. You had a group of people relying on you."

"I don't give a shit about those people! You were hurt! Don't you think I wanted to be with you?"

"I didn't mean it like that." It's all I can say. I didn't choose Oliver over Greg, I just didn't want to inconvenience him. Not once did I consider how it might look – how Greg would feel, or how it would embarrass him in front of the others that his own girlfriend would shun him.

Greg's eyes don't leave my face, but the fire inside of them dims slightly. For a second, he squeezes my hand back. "I'm not sleeping with Joanna," he sighs. "She's a friend, nothing more."

I believe him, but somehow nothing is fixed. Greg gets to his feet. "I should go."

"Please don't. Ally's on her way back – we can have some dinner and talk about this."

His eyes narrow as he considers it. Then they darken. "Who's bringing her home?"

"Oliver," I admit, and I know what he's going to say before he even says it.

"I can't stay right now, Emma.

"Yes, you can. I want you to stay."

He doesn't meet my eyes. "You need to get some rest. I'll call you tomorrow."

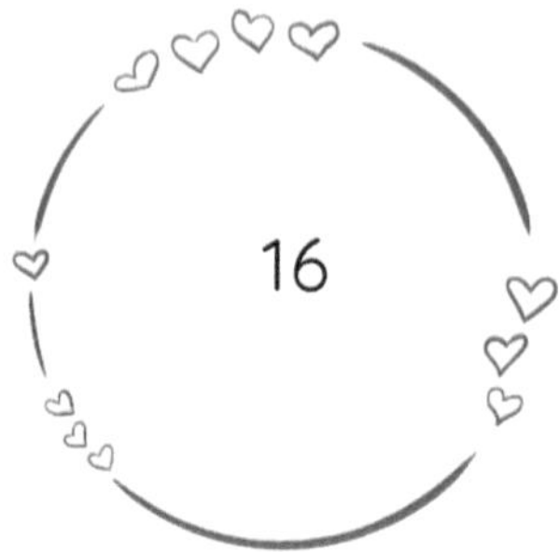

"It's a double," Oliver announces on Monday morning, setting an enormous paper cup on my desk. "I figured you might need it."

"You have no idea." I take a sip and burn the roof of my mouth.

"It's hot." Oliver is laughing, but I can't seem to locate my sense of humor. Greg didn't call yesterday. I'd spent the day on the sofa with Ally, watching cartoons and checking my phone every five minutes, but other than a few texts from Oliver to check if I was feeling better, the screen remained depressingly black.

"Do you want to grab lunch today?"

"I can't. I have a meeting with Greaves Dawson's at eleven."

He gives a low whistle. "Good luck."

"Thanks." I'm already rifling through my notes, and I barely notice when he gets up and leaves.

AT FIVE MINUTES TO ELEVEN, I'm ushered into a boardroom which is as impressive as it is intimidating. The table is twice the size of our own at Focus, and the marble floor is polished to a high sheen. I take a seat at the end of the table and pull out the proposal I've spent almost a week working on. When the door opens, an austere woman in a tailored two-piece suit stalks in. Her face is slightly familiar.

"Miss Johnson, I'm Joanna Meadon. I hope you don't mind, but I hijacked your meeting. Ultimately the decision is mine, so I let my associates off the hook." She extends her arm as I rise for the chair. "How's your head? That was quite a fall you had on Saturday."

I cringe, mortified that she witnessed it. I catch sight of her muscular calves, the sign of a true cyclist. She looks only a few years older than me, but her face is harder.

"I'm fine, thank you for asking. I guess cycling just isn't for me."

"It's not for everyone," she concedes drily. "Look, I'm going to level with you. The reason we reached out, is because you came highly recommended by Nanosec. By Greg," she adds meaningfully. "I know that the two of you have been seeing one another, but I've also known him long enough to know that he doesn't mix business and pleasure. He wouldn't recommend you if you weren't the best."

"I like to think I know what I'm doing," I reply. "I've had a look through your account history and I'm almost certain I could cut your expenditure by twenty percent, while still retaining your current rate of return."

"That's a very bold statement."

I raise my chin. I don't care if Greg referred me, he wasn't wrong. I'm good at my job, and I know what I can do.

"I can talk you through it, if I may?" Joanna lowers her eyes first.

It takes the better part of two hours before we are done.

"I'm impressed," Joanna admits. Despite the rocky start, I'm surprised to find that I like her. She's direct, but she's smart, and she doesn't mince her words. I hold my breath as she considers, her perfectly manicured fingers drumming on the smooth table top. Finally, she comes to a decision.

"We'll sign on with Focus. A six-month trial, with a possible two-year extension."

"Thank you. You won't be sorry. Although the projections I've made were based on a two-year period, I'm confident you'll see immediate results."

"I want to be very clear about one thing," she continues as if I haven't spoken. "We are signing on with *you*, specifically."

"I'm not sure I understand what you mean?"

"It's come to my attention that Oliver James was recently employed in your sales department."

"Yes...?" I draw out the word, not understanding where this is heading.

"Under no circumstances do I want Mr. James involved in our portfolio. I trust that won't present a problem?"

My mind reels. No sooner has she issued the instruction when it hits me. *Greg*. I can't believe he would stoop this low.

"Miss Meadon, I'm not sure what you have been told, but Oliver is a very valuable member of our team. To exclude him from a project of this magnitude—"

She cuts across me. "Despite what you may think, I don't base my decisions based on hearsay. I have my own reasons for not wanting Oliver James anywhere near my account." This time, I look away first. "Now," Joanna continues, "is this going to be a problem?"

"No," I admit, stifling the guilt that racks my chest. "I'll take care of it."

JACK IS EUPHORIC. Landing this account is the largest feather in Focus's cap since Nanosec came on board. Joanna and two of her directors visit Focus on Wednesday to sign the contract and the second they are out the door, he calls for champagne.

"Well done, Emma," he toasts. Most of the sales department is crammed into the boardroom, including Oliver, who gives me a high-five. I haven't told Jack about Joanna's condition yet, and my stomach is in knots. To top it off, I still haven't heard from Greg. Despite Joanna's insistence that it has nothing to do with him, I can't help but think that he somehow sabotaged Oliver out of spite. I've been so busy negotiating the final terms of this contract that I haven't had a moment to get in touch with him about it, but now that it's wrapped up, the sense of urgency to do so is overwhelming.

"I just need to make a quick call," I tell Jack.

"Nonsense! This is your victory party, everything else can wait!"

"I just need to check on Alyssa," I say, pulling the concerned parent card. "I won't be long."

I closet myself in my office and dial Greg's number. It almost rings off, and for a dreaded heartbeat I think he's not going to answer, but he does.

"Emma?"

"Hi." Now that I've got him on the line, I can't seem to find the right words.

"I just got off the phone with Joanna," Greg tells me, "I believe congratulations are in order."

The mention of her brings me back to the issue at hand. "We need to talk."

"You're damn right we do, but I was under the impression you didn't want to talk to me."

What? "I just... look, I really need to see you. Could I swing by after work?"

"I don't think this can wait. Can you come past my office?"

"Of course."

"I'll see you shortly." he disconnects, and I quickly send a text to my mom to let her know that I'll be late fetching Alyssa.

I've just hit send when Oliver's head appears around my door. "Everything okay?"

"Actually, no. Can you come in here for a second? There's something I need to tell you."

17

"She didn't say why?" Oliver's eyes are wide, and he shifts uncomfortably in his seat. He's taken the news badly, but I can't blame him. Finding out that one of the biggest brands in the country has specifically requested you be excluded from their account is a bitter pill to swallow, especially when you're trying to build a reputation in corporate advertising.

"I'm going to sort this out," I promise. "I don't know for sure, but I think that maybe Greg... well, he and Joanna are friends, and he's not your biggest fan."

"You think Greg did this?" His voice is low and furious.

"I don't know for sure. I'm heading over to see him, and I promise I'll get to the bottom of this. I'll sort it out. If it is him, I mean."

"What else could it be, Emma?" he's yelling now.

"Oliver, calm down!"

He runs his hands through his hair. "I'm sorry. It's just, well, this is a lot, you know?"

"I know." I nod in sympathy. "Look, before I head out, is there any reason that Joanna Meadon would want you excluded. Anything you can think of? You came from SalesCom, right? Did you ever have any dealings with Greaves before?"

"No. SalesCom is a tiny fish in a very large pond. They didn't have the resources to handle an account this size."

"She was insistent that this was her decision. Think, Oliver."

"I am thinking!" his eyes dart around the room before settling on my face. "Do you think I did this?"

"I'm not saying that."

"Well, you're certainly not saying that your boyfriend is the villain here. Does Jack know?"

"No, I haven't told him yet."

"This could ruin my career, Emma."

I knead my temples. "Look, let's not panic just yet." I glance at my watch. "I'm going to see Greg now, this can't wait. Let me go and tell Jack – I'll tell him there's an emergency at home. I'll be right back."

He sinks onto the chair opposite my desk and nods bleakly. As I pass, I place my hand on his shoulder. "It's going to be okay, Oliver."

When I return for my things, he's still slumped in the chair.

"What did Jack say?"

"That we'll pick this up tomorrow. Look, go home. Try to relax. I'll call you as soon as I leave Nanosec."

"You're going to his office?"

"Yes."

"And you'll call me?"

"Of course. Just as soon as I'm done." I feel terrible, leaving him in this state, but the best way to help him is to get to the bottom of this.

GREG IS in a meeting when I arrive, so I wait in reception while Tracey casts dark glances in my direction.

"I'm not sure how long Mr. Daniels will be," she says pointedly. "And without an appointment..."

"He's expecting me," I fire back.

As if on cue, Greg's office doors open. He gestures me in while Tracey walks his guests to the elevators.

"That will be all, Tracey," he tells her on his way back. "You can pack up and head home."

I wait until the doors are closed before I begin.

"I saw Joanna."

"I heard." He walks around his desk and focuses on his laptop. "She was very impressed."

There's no easy way to have this conversation, so I dive right in.

"She asked me to exclude Oliver from all dealings with Greaves."

His eyes meet mine over the laptop. "And you were surprised?"

His words stop me in my tracks. "Did you have something to do with this?"

"Emma, I don't know what's going on with you, but I'd think, given the information I sent you, that you'd have taken some action yourself. I get that you're angry with me, but—"

"What information?"

His head jerks up. "You didn't get my emails?"

"Greg, I haven't heard from you since you walked out on Saturday."

"Jesus, Emma, you're not serious."

I take a step back. "Why don't you just tell me what is going on?"

"I did some digging over the weekend. It seems your friend Oliver has had a number of near-misses with the law over the past three years."

"What?"

"Several women have laid charges of assault against him. One even claimed he was stalking her." He scans his screen. "A Juliana Reynolds – has he ever mentioned that name to you?"

"No." My addled brain doesn't seem to be firing on all cylinders. "Oliver would never... if he'd committed a criminal offense, personnel would have picked it up."

"That's the thing, he was never convicted. All charges were withdrawn."

"This can't be true. Oliver's a good guy. How do you know these women weren't just trying to blackmail him, or..." I trail off, unable to think of a single reason why anyone would do that.

"I tracked down his ex-wife, Simone James."

"Simone?" I shake my head. "No, that can't be right. Simone is some woman he dated, she's been stalking him, not the other way around."

"Simone was with Oliver five years, married only one of those. She says he's mentally unstable. He's harassed her for years since their divorce, but in the past few months he's left her alone. She was concerned – she thought perhaps he'd turned his attention to someone new." He gives me a pointed look.

"This is crazy. He's never done anything to raise any flags. He's my *friend*, Greg."

"I know he is. Which is why I didn't report this to Jack, or the authorities, not without concrete proof." He frowns at his screen. "That's why I sent it to you instead."

"I haven't received anything from you."

"It's right here!" he swivels his laptop to show me the screen. Three emails, all in his outbox, addressed to me.

"I've been busy, maybe I missed them." It's a hollow claim. I wouldn't miss an email from Greg. But I had been away from my desk for hours at a time, working through the Greaves contract. My stomach contracts. "Someone must've deleted them."

"Did someone screen my calls, too?"

"What?"

"I've been trying to call you for three days, Emma."

"That's impossible. I would've seen missed calls from you." I don't add that I'd been checking for his name every five minutes.

"Check your register."

I do, to find dozens of calls from Greg's number.

"What the hell?" Greg is already dialing. He puts his phone on speaker, and we both listen to the sound of dialed ringing. My phone stays silent.

"He must've blocked my number." Greg is on his feet. "Emma, this is serious. If he's tampered with your phone and your emails, we need to go to the police. And we need to alert Jack, too."

I nod, struck dumb with the revelation that Oliver might really be who Greg says he is.

"I need to check in with my parents – to let them know what's happening."

"You can call on the way."

We're already in the elevator when my mom answers. "Hey love, are you done already?"

"No, not yet. Mom, something's happened. My friend Oliver – he's, well, he might be dangerous. I need you to keep Alyssa tonight, can you do that?"

"Alyssa?" her voice is a horrified whimper. "Emma, Oliver picked Alyssa up a few minutes ago. You texted me to let me know he was coming!"

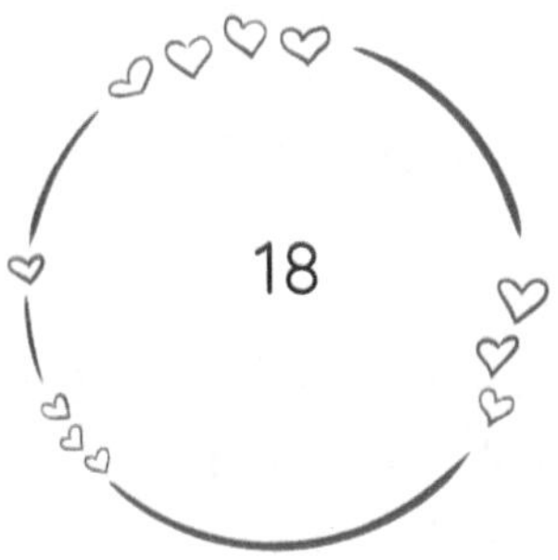

Someone must be looking over me because every light is green as we race toward Oliver's apartment. Greg is on the phone to the cops, explaining what's happened. I've tried Oliver's cell, but he's switched it off. Jack says that nobody has seen him since I left, but he's alerted security and that if Oliver tries to enter the building, he'll be detained.

"What else can I do?" he asks before I disconnect.

"Could you pull his files, try to find any alternate address?"

"I'm on it. I'll call you if I find anything."

Greg finishes up his call at the same time. "They've put out an alert. They're sending someone over to the house too, we'll meet them there." He falls silent and then slams his hands on the wheel. "Dammit! I should've just come to see you."

"Why didn't you?"

He hangs his head. "Male pride? I don't know, Emma. I had suspicions but nothing concrete. I thought you were avoiding me. I was pissed off. Put it down to a number of stupid reasons."

"You did try to warn me." It's little consolation, but it's all I can offer. A strange calm has settled over me. Inside, I am spinning out of control, my fear for Alyssa threatening to overwhelm me, but a combination of adrenalin and determination is keeping me going.

"I didn't think it was this serious," Greg says, apology in every word.

"I'm going to kill him," I say softly. "If we find them, I am going to kill him with my bare hands."

"*When* we find them," he corrects, "I'll help you."

The police arrive at Oliver's apartment first. They go in ahead of us, but I already know he's not here. I've visited only a few times in the past few months, but I always thought it was a happy apartment. Now, something heavy hangs in the air. A sense of wrongness. How could I have been so blind? Like a film reel, I keep playing all our interactions over and over in my head, trying to pinpoint where I went wrong. There was the odd look, gesture, a flash of anger that seemed out of place but that I could explain away at the time.

"Where the hell is my daughter!" Max's voice penetrates my dark musing, and I rush back into the hall to find him grappling with a police officer who is trying to stop him from coming inside.

"Let him go!" I yell, skidding a halt beside them. Greg pulls me back, just in time to avoid getting an elbow in the face. "That's my ex-husband – he's Alyssa's father!" I yell at the policeman. He releases Max immediately.

"Where is she, Emma?" Max's eyes are frantic and fearful, but there's no trace of the redness which accompanies his drinking.

"I don't know, Max. Oliver fetched her from my folks – he sent a text from my phone when I wasn't looking – but I have no idea where he could've taken her."

"How did this happen? How did he get your phone in the first place, and why in God's name would your parents let her go off with some stranger?"

"He's not a stranger. He's picked her up for me a few times when I've run late, and my parents have met him multiple times. As for my phone, I have no idea. He must've texted when I left him alone in my office just before I left."

"This is your fault!"

I open my mouth to deny it, but no words come out.

"I'm sorry," I manage, before Greg intercepts.

"I'm calling Simone," he says. "She's Oliver's ex-wife," he explains to Max. "She might know where he would go."

My phone rings. I snatch it up and almost pass out with relief when I see Oliver's number.

"Oliver!"

"Hey, Emma." He sounds so normal, so unconcerned, that for a second I wonder if this has all been a terrible misunderstanding.

"Where's Alyssa?" Greg and Max have frozen beside me, hanging on every word. I watch as Greg gestures the nearest policeman over and signs to him that Oliver is on the phone.

"I should've left when I saw his emails," Oliver says, and I hear it then, the touch of madness lurking below the cool exterior. "I wanted to, but I thought I'd have more time to make you see."

"Make me see what, Oliver? Where is my daughter?" Through the crippling terror, I hear a sound in the background that seems amplified because I know it so well. My eyes widen as I turn to Greg. *Southside Mall,* I mouth. I'd know the sound of that arcade game anywhere, Alyssa plays it every time we go shopping.

Max is already moving. Keeping my voice calm, I follow him down the stairs while Greg hastily explains to the cops what's going on.

"Where is she?" I say into the phone, keeping up pretenses. "Why did you take her? Please, Oliver, she's only a little girl. She has nothing to do with this. Please bring her back. I won't tell anyone, I promise." I raise my voice at the end, trying to mask the sound of the car door closing.

Max already has the engine running when Greg tears out of the lobby. I hit the mute button as he leaps into the back seat.

"I'm not going to hurt her, Emma. I only wanted you to hear me out."

"I'm listening! I'll come to you, we can sit down and have a drink. You can explain it all, but please let me get Alyssa home first."

"Not until you promise you won't call the cops."

"Why would I do that? You're my friend, Oliver."

"What about the lies your boyfriend told you about me?"

"Greg?" I force as much disdain into my voice as I can. "I didn't even give him the chance. He admitted that he's been seeing Joanna, would you believe it. As far as I'm concerned, he can go to hell."

Max gives Greg a confused look over his shoulder, but Greg just shakes his head and gestures for me to keep going.

"Why did you take Ally?" I ask. "Were you trying to help me out? I know you expected I might be late?"

I've given him an easy out, and he seizes it. "You know I'd do anything for you, Emma."

"I know." I force a laugh. "God knows I'd never survive at the office without your daily coffee delivery. I don't know what Greg is trying to do, but he's not going to succeed."

"He really slept with her?"

I lower my voice. "He really did."

"God, Em, that sucks. I'm sorry."

It blows my mind how quickly he's slipped back into the old familiarity. The son of a bitch has taken my daughter and yet he's talking to me as if we're still the best of friends.

"Tell me about it. My taste in men sucks." The irony of that statement, given that two of those choices are currently in the car with me, on a mission to save my daughter, is almost laughable.

"Where are you, Oliver? I'll come to you and we can sit down and talk about it. I need a shoulder to cry on."

We've arrived at the mall and my adrenalin spikes. There are loads of people here, he'll hear it if I get out of the car. In the background on Oliver's side, I hear Alyssa's voice and my chest constricts.

"Can I speak to her?"

"She's fine."

"I know she is. I know you'd never hurt her. I just want to hear her voice – I've been so worried."

He gives no indication that he's going to do it, but the second Ally's breathless voice comes down the line, I'm moving, launching out of the car and sprinting toward the arcade, Greg and Max right beside me.

"Mommy," Alyssa whines.

"Hey, baby! Are you having fun?"

"I want to come ho"

"There, are you happy?" Oliver demands. I cringe as a group of teenagers rushes past, gossiping at the top of their voices. Oliver gives a bellow of rage and cuts the call.

"He knows!" I yell, pushing my body even faster. "He knows we're here!"

Greg bolts through the crowd, cutting a path for me and Max. I keep my head down and sprint after him, scanning the sea of faces.

Greg gets there first. Oliver is trying to drag Alyssa out of one of the back exits when Greg's fist thunders toward his face. He spins a full 360 degrees and drops Ally. I snatch her up, cradling her to my chest. She's crying, and I cover her face as Greg hits Oliver again. Then Max is there, leaping on top of Oliver as he goes down and landing blow after blow every place he can reach.

It happens so quickly I can barely keep up. I'm stroking Alyssa's back, her hair, and smothering her with kisses, desperate to reassure myself that she's unharmed. The police arrive and haul Greg and Max off Oliver, who is whimpering in pain and fear.

His eyes meet mine, and I wonder how it's possible to hate someone as much as I hate him right now. He sees it and his bloody mouth opens.

"Emma." It's a plea. Over Alyssa's head, I mouth three words so only he can see. *Go fuck yourself.*

. . .

IT'S A LONG NIGHT. My parents meet us at the police station where we all have our statements taken. I'm sitting in the waiting room with Alyssa on my knee while Greg finishes up giving his account of events when a mousy-haired, long-legged woman walks in. Her doe-eyes are wide and fearful. I know instinctively who she is.

"Mom, take Ally for me, please." I get to my feet and walk forward to meet her. "You must be Simone." She can't seem to focus on anything, her eyes scanning the room. "I'm Emma," I say, holding out my hand.

Her eyes find mine. "Are you her?"

"I am."

She exhales a sigh of relief. "I wanted to warn you, but he wouldn't tell me who you were. And he wouldn't take any of my calls."

It strikes me that I, myself, helped Oliver's cause. I helped him screen this woman when all she wanted to do was help me.

"Everything happened so quickly," I say. "One minute he was fine, the next..." I swallow down the lump in my throat. "He took my daughter."

She follows the line of my arm to see Alyssa snuggling into my mother's chest. Her eyes look more, rather than less terrified.

"That's how it is with him," she whispers. "Sometimes I used to think I was the crazy one. He's an amazing man, but then..." she pauses, gathering herself. "His medication helped, but he refused to stay on it."

I take her hand. "It's okay. You don't have to talk about it."

"Where is he?"

"He's been taken into custody. The officer in charge says he'll be convicted unless there's a medical reason to have him committed. Either way, he's not going to hurt anyone, ever again."

Her legs are trembling. "He's sick. He doesn't mean it, but when he's off his meds, he can't control himself. I tried to help him, I..." she takes a deep breath. "I tried."

"Like you said, he's sick."

"He wouldn't hurt anyone if he could help it."

I stare up at her, at the compassion and sadness reflected in her brown eyes.

"My mother used to say that," I say.

EPILOGUE

It's been three months since Oliver was arrested. He's currently undergoing treatment for his mental health issues. I don't know how long he'll be there, or whether he'll serve jail time after, and I don't care. Simone was right – he is sick, but he's also a coward. He won't come near me or my family again, and, if he does, I'll be ready for him.

That said, he'd need to get through Greg's security system first. Ally and I moved in with Greg six weeks ago. It'll take some getting used to. I haven't sold my house yet. I did, however, sell the bicycle. Greg's quite content with my new creed to keep the cardio in the bedroom.

Max is still sober. He brought his new girlfriend around for a barbecue last weekend. She's nice enough to treat Ally well, but not nice enough to take any nonsense. She'll keep Max on the straight and narrow, not that I think he needs it.

I haven't seen or heard from Megan. She didn't even make contact after what happened. Last I heard, she'd been dismissed from Carter & Boyd for inappropriate conduct. I'm not sure what she did, but I have my suspicions.

. . .

THE END

ABOUT THE AUTHOR

Rachel Rhodes is a pseudonym for award-winning author, copywriter, and lover of the written word, Melissa Delport. She is published in both S.A and the U.S.A and offers professional copywriting services and author coaching.

For ten years she owned and operated her own specialized logistics company until she woke up one morning and decided it was time to put her English degree to good use.

Melissa lives with her husband and three teenagers, none of whom take her seriously.

She also writes romantic suspense as Lissa Del and contemporary romance as Rachel Rhodes.

For more information, visit www.melissadelport.com

ALSO BY RACHEL RHODES

ROMANCE & ROMANTIC COMEDY (as Rachel Rhodes)

Awkward in Print

Awkward Abroad

Awkward Infidelity

Awkward in Trouble

CONTEMPORARY WOMENS FICTION (as Lissa Del)

Rainfall

Riven

A Life Made of Lava

URBAN FANTASY

GUARDIANS OF SUMMERFELD SERIES

The Cathedral of Cliffdale (Book 1)

The Fight of the Fallen (Book 2)

The Hope of Hawkstone (Book 3)

The Balance of the Blood (Book 4)

Full Series Boxed Set (Books 1-4)

SHADOW MAGIC SERIES

The Witchborn Curse (Book 1)

The Shadow Huntress (Book 2)

The Charmed Quarter (Book 3)

The Rogue Coven (Book 4)

The Darkest Realm (Book 5)

The Hybrid's Fate (Book 6)

Full Series Boxed Set (Books 1-6)

THE TRAVELER DUOLOGY

The Traveler (Book 1)

The Survivor (Book 1.5)

The Saviour (Book 2)

TIME TRAVEL FANTASY

The Clock Keeper

DYSTOPIAN

THE LEGACY TRILOGY

The Legacy (Legacy Trilogy Book 1)

The Legion (Legacy Trilogy Book 2)

The Legend (Legacy Trilogy Book 3)

ANTHOLOGIES

The Space Between Dreams & Chaos

The Space Between Magic & Mayhem

www.ingramcontent.com/pod-product-compliance
Lightning Source LLC
Chambersburg PA
CBHW020912310726
48980CB00011B/856/J

* 9 7 8 0 6 3 9 8 4 4 8 7 9 *